REFUSAL

Soazig Aaron was born in Rennes. She lived in Paris for several years, working in a bookshop, and now lives in Brittany. For this, her first novel (published in France as *Le non de Klara*), she was awarded the Prix Emmanuel-Roblès and a Goncourt scholarship.

Barbara Bray has translated works by Duras, Pinget, Sartre, Robbe-Grillet and Flaubert and has won many prizes for her translations, including, on four occasions, the George Scott-Moncrieff Prize for translation from the French. She is currently working on a personal memoir of Samuel Beckett which is to be published by Harvill Secker.

D0540307

SOAZIG AARON

Refusal

TRANSLATED FROM THE FRENCH BY
Barbara Bray

VINTAGE BOOKS
London

Published by Vintage 2008

1 3 5 7 9 10 8 6 4 2

Copyright © Soazig Aaron and Maurice Nadeau 2002
English translation copyright © Barbara Bray 2007

Soazig Aaron has asserted her right under the Copyright, Designs
and Patents Act 1988 to be identified as the author of this work

The quotations reproduced on p. vii are from:
Robert Pinget, *Traces of Ink*, Red Dust, Inc., 2000, translated by Barbara Wright
Marina Tsvetayeva, Poem 8, dated 15 March-11 May 1939, in *Poems to Czech.
March*, cited in Irma Kudrova, *The Death of a Poet*, Duckworth, 2004,
translated by Mary Ann Szporluk

First published with the title *Le non de Klara* by Maurice Nadeau

First published in Great Britain in 2007 by
Harvill Secker
Random House, 20 Vauxhall Bridge Road,
London SW1V 2SA

www.vintage-books.co.uk

Addresses for companies within The Random House Group Limited can be
found at: www.randomhouse.co.uk/offices.htm

The Random House Group Limited Reg. No. 954009

A CIP catalogue record for this book
is available from the British Library

ISBN 9780099466659

This book is supported by the French Ministry of Foreign Affairs, as part of the
Burgess Programme run by the Cultural Department of the French
Embassy in London

Liberté • Égalité • Fraternité
RÉPUBLIQUE FRANÇAISE

Printed and bound in Great Britain by
CPI Cox & Wyman, Reading, RG1 8EX

TO

Morgan

TO

Yann

Only when you have spoken out already
have you the right to be silent.

Robert Pinget *Traces of Ink*

There is just one answer to your
Senseless world – refusal.

Marina Tsvetayeva

Sunday, July 29, 1945

Klara's back. There, it's down in black and white. I have to write it down to make it more real and make myself believe it. For three days I haven't been certain of anything. Klara's back. It's lucky I've got this exercise-book handy, even with its poor wartime paper. But for it, everything would sink without trace, *I* would sink without trace.

We do speak; yes. To each other; among the three of us.
  Alban and I.
  Klara and I.
  Alban and Klara.
  Alban, Klara and I.
  Even so, I can't grasp it.
  Klara's back. Among the last of them, Klara's back.
  Klara, Klara, Klara.
  I keep saying the name over and over to make sure it really is Klara, our friend Klara, my friend Klara, my brother's wife, Victoire's mother.
  Since Friday, Alban and I have been taking it in turns to be with her, here in the rue Richer. She refuses to see

Victoire, her little girl, or Agathe, who took Victoire in and saved her life in July '42.

It's as if there were a thick sheet of ice between us. Not that what she says doesn't make sense, but there's an aura of madness around her. Sometimes she gabbles, sometimes she speaks slowly and evenly. But she's never calm for a moment, even though her tone of voice never varies. She keeps tormenting the cushion in the corner of the divan, or else paces around the sitting-room. She's never still.

It's strange, though, that I should have gone to the Lutétia* on Thursday. There wasn't much hope left by then. Almost all of them were back. But I happened to be near the rue de Sèvres and thought I might as well drop in—you never know. And I think now that I'd still have kept going back for a long time if I hadn't found out what had become of her. I'd registered all the necessary details about ourselves with the authorities, I'd left Klara's own name and photograph, but in order to be sure I was doing everything possible I did call in regularly, if only on the chance of meeting others who might have known her. Lots of people do that, still going on hoping. They all say you never know, just as I used to do.

~

*[Tr. The Lutétia, a large hotel in the boulevard Raspail, still fashionable today, which was used as a clearing-house around the end of World War II for refugees from German war-zones, ex-prisoners of war, ex-deportees and survivors from the Nazi concentration camps.]

But as soon as I was in the foyer I didn't think any more. I *felt* Klara was there . . . She was there. I couldn't see her, but she was there. It was very strange. I went hot and cold, my heart started pounding, I couldn't keep my hands from shaking. Everyone knows the feeling.

The only other people there were two women sitting down and a young man standing, a small, odd-looking fellow wearing a jacket too big for him but buttoned up tight, together with rather crumpled black trousers over a pair of climbing boots. He was standing astride a little red suitcase. On the floor to one side of him was what looked like some kind of black animal, a dog lying down perhaps. The boy himself had very short fair hair, smooth hollow cheeks and huge eyes; they often do have huge eyes. Be that as it may, this particular pair were looking at me, had perhaps been fixed on me for some time. It was Klara. She didn't move. I remember her eyes. Fixed, unwavering. Everyone says it's by their eyes, something in their eyes, that you recognise them. I didn't believe it. The eyes of all those I've seen come back—those in bad shape, precisely those you don't recognise—are empty, empty, so empty they look deep. So you don't know what to make of it.

All this could have lasted some time. I remember feeling rooted to the spot, incapable of thought. My legs, however, must have taken the steps necessary for me to take her in my arms. But she stood completely stiff. She let me kiss her once, but I didn't try again: her whole body was saying no.

I must have blurted out 'Klara, Klara,' that's all. It might have been foolish, ridiculous even. I could have been mistaken, the young man might have thought I was crazy, and said nothing. But I didn't have time to think about it, because Klara said, 'Hallo, Angélika. How are you?' Her voice was rough and rasping. I remembered her as having a voice that was gentle and sweet: gentle Klara, headstrong Klara, but gentle too.

I can hear her walking about in the living-room as I write. She thinks I'm asleep. *She* never sleeps. She'll doze on the divan for a quarter of an hour or so from time to time, then there's a sort of cry, not very loud, and immediately afterwards she starts walking about again. I can hear her despite the fact that there's a corridor between the two rooms. The bare floor is too noisy; I'll bring some rugs over from Trocadéro. She won't have the bedroom next to the living-room, or mine either, though it doesn't overlook the street and is quieter.

I hadn't tried to imagine how things might turn out, so I was unprepared, and now that she was there *she* didn't help. My hands were still trembling and my teeth were beginning to chatter. Then she bent down and picked up the little red case and the dog, which was really a big black coat. 'Let's go,' she said. Her voice was toneless, uninflected, I didn't know how to react. But I said, 'First we must tell someone. There are formalities to be gone through at the reception centre.' She said, 'Don't bother—they've given me enough trouble already.' I knew, I felt, that this wasn't the old Klara, but puzzled by her attitude, no doubt a mixture of recklessness, indifference, and resentment, I pulled myself together and said, as I might have said in the old days: 'You wait for me outside if you like—I'll see to it.'

So she left, and I found a suitable official to whom to explain that Klara Schwarz-Roth was coming with me: she was my sister-in-law. We'd left our names and addresses months ago, my husband and I, Dr Naël and Solange Blanc, but hadn't had any notification of her return. The girl at the desk looked through all her lists but couldn't find Klara's name anywhere—ours were there, but not hers. I left, followed by the girl. Klara herself just stood gazing at the boulevard Raspail. 'They can't find your name, Klara,' I said. Without even turning round, she said, 'Sarah Adler.' The girl said, 'Oh, so *that's* you, is it?!' The girl and I went back and looked at the list again, and Sarah Adler was on it. I felt rather embarrassed, until, turning round, I saw Klara shrug her shoulders. That struck me as funny, and I almost wanted to laugh. In '38 all three of us used to do our best to be like the French.

The girl said, 'I don't think she's very easy to deal with.' I said, 'Isn't she? How long has she been here?' It said on the list that she'd come back from Auschwitz on Monday July 16. But none of the details fitted together. In the normal way she would have been here at least two months, but she's not very cooperative, and as on top of that she lied about who she was, that made for even more confusion. I said, 'Adler's her father's surname, so only the given name is false, if that's how you want to look at it. I don't know you, but like you I came to work here as a volunteer in April and May, and Dr Naël, my husband, still comes when he can, to examine the ex-prisoners when they arrive. Klara's not a habitual liar, but she must have her reasons. You know as well as I do how odd these people are.' The girl relaxed. 'I can't tell you any more myself—one of my colleagues knows the case better. But we'll have to get the whole story straightened out, you know, to give her an identity card and so on, and to find out what benefits she's entitled to.' I promised to cooperate.

Alban will go in tomorrow. Klara won't do anything.

I went back to her. She hadn't moved; the little red case and the coat that looked like a dog were still by her feet. I said, 'Sorry, Klara, but it had to be done. Now we'll get a taxi and go home. Are you feeling all right? Can I carry something for you?'

'No. I'm all right. Where *is* home? You've moved, haven't you?'

'Have you been to the rue Richer?'

'Yes. There wasn't anyone there. The shutter things were closed.'

'Alban and I and Victoire live at Trocadéro these days. Victoire's a big girl now. She's a darling—I'm sure you'll be pleased with her.'

By then we were out on the boulevard, with Klara stepping out doggedly beside me. There weren't many people around in the streets. Klara's heavy shoes thudded on the heated surface of the pavement. She suddenly halted and said, 'Non, che ne ne feux pas.' 'No, I don't want to.' That was when I remembered that she'd never lost her German accent, either in French or in English; I hadn't remembered her slow way of speaking, either. To gain time, and because I thought there might be some language difficulty, I said, 'Would you rather we spoke German?' She said, 'No, never again, and I don't vant to see the child, either.' And she put down her little red case and the dog-like coat and stood still, just shaking her little bird-like head and repeating 'No, no, no, I don't vant to see the child, either.'

I had to make a decision. Klara was in a mood to refuse everything, and scared me because she was no longer the old Klara. And I was going to have to get used to it. I suggested we go to a café and talk—she must have something to eat and drink, anyway. Must, must, must. How many 'musts' was I going to have to shoulder from now on!

I found an inconspicuous table at the back of the café. I was afraid people would stare at Klara—she looked so strange.

Klara's first words in the café: 'So you see, I'm back.'

'But it's been a long time. Three years,' I said.

'But you see, people do come back . . . I've been wandering about all over the place since March—Cracow, Prague, Linz, Berlin and wherever else I could in Germany. I was inspecting my home. The others were in a hurry to get back, but I wasn't. They are returning to their own countries, but I've left mine for the last time. And here I am.'

'The girl at the Lutétia said you'd been back for over a week. Why, Klara? . . . Why didn't you get in touch?'

'I didn't know where you were. And I wanted to see Paris again on my own. That takes time. I used to stay in the reception-hall at the Lutétia for an hour every afternoon, then leave. Today I still had half an hour to wait.'

'In the rue Lafayette there's Agathe and your own apartment. Agathe could have . . .'

'No.'

'Don't you want to see Agathe again either?'

'No.'

'All this is going to make things difficult.'

'Tell her I've still got that big pin of hers. Look!'

She showed me a safety-pin inside her jacket, under the collar.

'You've kept it for three years?'

'Yes. Tell her it's always come in useful; and so has something else, some last words, tell her—something very beautiful that I'll tell *you* later on—but I don't want to see *her*.'

'And Victoire, Klara—what are we going to do about her? She's a pretty, merry little girl. You can't imagine how sweet and funny she is, a real chatterbox, absolutely charming, Klara. She speaks very well and has fair, curly hair just like you used to have.'

'And she's called Victoire now?'

'Yes, I changed it from Vera, ten days after . . . when I registered her in my own new name, Blanc, and Alban recognised her as his too, to make it safer. At the same time, his parents let us have the Trocadéro apartment—the one in the rue Henri-Martin—because it was safer. They went to live in the country.'

'Victoire's good—I used to say "qui vivra verra"—time will tell, those who live will see what happens—so I named her Vera. And you called her Victoire—those who live will see victory. That's good. But *I*'m dead, and the little girl you're talking about has got a mother and father already. She's lucky. And one doesn't deprive anyone of their luck.'

'You'll come to us then, Klara? Victoire is at Agathe's. That'll do for tonight.'

'Yes, if the child's not there I'll come with you. Otherwise I'll go back to the hotel. That's quite possible, and anyway it's of no importance.'

While we were talking, the waiter came and took our order.

She said: 'I'd like a coffee.'

I said: 'The same for me too, please, monsieur.'

With some difficulty I managed to get through to Alban on the phone at work.

I'm trying to write this all down calmly in order to sort out my thoughts a little, but it's not easy because I had so many other things on my mind when it happened. Victoire was one big problem, but there was also the ever-present question of Rainer. The situation was so delicate it didn't occur to me to wonder why Klara showed no concern about him. It should have struck me as odd, because his name was always at the back of my own mind, though I didn't say anything either. It's only now I realise how peculiar that was. But everything was peculiar.

I was still in such a state of shock that as we talked in the café I didn't show any reaction to the surprises I felt, the questions that crowded in on me, or those that should have but didn't. It was the same as with Klara's accent, which struck me only suddenly, after we'd already exchanged a few sentences.

On top of all that, as I now realise, I was also studying Klara herself. Taking her in, rather. She might have been a boy of sixteen, a woman of forty, anything—someone whose relation to time was not clear, so you might say she spanned all ages and all fashions, and became neutral, belonging to none.

Alban sounded very happy on the phone.

'No!' he said. 'How is she? Is she all right?' I said, 'Yes, but not as you might think. She's very, very thin, but I expect you've seen worse. She's odd, though—I'll tell you the strangest thing right away. She doesn't want to see Victoire or Agathe—what shall we do?' He's a fast thinker, but he couldn't help letting out a gasp. 'Oh!' I heard him say, 'Oh—well, I'll go round to Agathe's and ask her to hold on to Victoire for tonight. I'll be leaving here in an hour, we'll have Klara at our place this evening, and then we'll think what to do later. Are you all right, Lika? We shall both have to be strong, my love. It's tough, eh? But you know I'll be here, I *am* here. I'll get something for dinner, if you like—we'll do her proud.' I said, 'You think that's what we should do?' and added very quickly, 'Thanks, thanks, it does me good just to hear you—I'm still a bit lost.'

Monday, July 30, 1945

We separated quite early this evening. I said I wanted to go to bed, but I can't sleep, so I go on writing, like yesterday. At the moment I can't hear her. Before we separated she told me, 'I never had nightmares *there*. Now, here, I have them all the time. Here, and all through the journey from Poland. In the middle of the real nightmare, no nightmares. Here, nightmares all the time. Every night I live in the heart of the nightmare.'

On Saturday I had a long conversation with Agathe. She was shattered. At first she was so angry she almost shouted. 'So *we*, we guarded her treasure for her, we took risks, especially you two, but I as well, and my parents, and Alban's parents, we were all ready to do it, or to take over from you if necessary, and now *she* suddenly says, "I don't want your treasure!" It's crazy, *she's* crazy!' Afterwards she calmed down. Agathe is the soul of decency. 'Yes,' she said, 'but *we* love the treasure too, and we were glad to take risks. So there'll be no complaining—I was just being stupid.' All in all, she's more hurt than angry. It's the business about

Victoire that shocks her most. Her own maternal instincts are so strong she can't understand it. 'I have to admit such a thing can happen,' she says, 'but I find it hard to believe.' Yet she was the first to rejoice, and to put her finger on what we all felt deep down—at least I'm sure *I* did, and seeing how Alban was with Victoire right from the beginning, it must have been the same with him. Yes, we're not going to lose Victoire after all! And perhaps it's Agathe who'll help us to look on the bright side in general.

I asked her about the safety-pin. With tears in her eyes, she kept saying, 'But what have they done to her? What have they done to her? Klara's so sweet—she was my friend. It was she who took all my best photos. And how we all used to laugh together, and at Barbery with Alban and you and Rainer and Adrien and Frédéric too. That was before the war, and even in '40 we still laughed a bit. And why did she go and register? We all told her not to. But what *is* this life of Klara's? Rainer's dead, and she's back, and now she's like this—it's too stupid, too stupid.' I asked, 'And what was the last thing you said to her? She told me you said something very beautiful.'

Agathe: 'Something very beautiful!? . . . I don't know. I remember that Victoire and Isidore were sleeping together head to toe in the little bed at my place, and what I was most anxious about was that the other two idiots should leave Klara's key with me so that I could salvage her belongings. And that's what we did together afterwards, with her cameras, her files, her mother's jewellery, and Victoire and

Rainer's things . . . Something very beautiful? . . . I don't remember. I was in such a state. Perhaps it was when I gave her the safety-pin—people do ridiculous things at such times. I didn't remember about the safety-pin, so as for saying something beautiful . . . anything's possible, Lika, it can happen to anyone.'

I kissed Agathe then, because it was so good to hear her, and as I hugged her I laughed because it was comical that she should apologise for supposedly having said something beautiful.

Afterwards we talked again about the good times we'd all had together, especially at Barbery, her parents' place. They helped us to manage during the war. Antoine even started growing things on the lawn he'd been so proud of. After all, he used to say, there is a war on. With what remained of his architect's materials he built on a little room near the attic. In the evening he would make grand plans for the future kitchen garden. The idea was more impressive than the reality, but the vegetables accommodatingly grew in spite of everything, and Adeline's soups! . . . She kept hens and rabbits, and the two of them bought a nanny-goat—she was stolen only last year . . . The eggs and milk were mainly for the children after '43. Antoine and Adeline learned as they went along. They kept busy all the time to distract themselves from their anxieties.

When we went there, we helped. The boys with Antoine, the girls with Adeline. Agathe taught us how to make patterns. Adeline said we must learn to cut out and sew, turn collars, patch and mend. Agathe had magical powers. She could do whatever she liked with any kind of material. Klara was hopeless with her hands, so she took photographs. I could have done better myself, but I had no patience.

For Christmas '41 we had a chicken for dinner, with potatoes from the lawn, and an apple tart flavoured with some old cinnamon from before the war. It was gorgeous. We were all still there then. In the evening, Rainer played Chopin waltzes and some short pieces by Brahms. Antoine and Klara and Alban and Agathe danced. We talked of everything except what we were doing in Paris, about which we were silent out of both modesty and prudence, and to keep these rare moments happy, like before the war. It was doing us good, we knew.

After every meal they used to say, 'One more . . .' They didn't finish the sentence out of consideration for us three, but Alban told us what it meant, and we too used to say 'One more . . .' and laugh. '41, '42, '43, '44—all years of anguish. Rainer, Klara, Adrien, Frédéric—all gone, for different reasons. Those who were left were Alban and me, and Agathe and her parents looking after Isidore and Victoire, the babies who have since grown up. So have we.

Now we're without Rainer and Frédéric. Adrien came back with one eye missing. He says it's cheap at the price considering what he went through. He's no longer the student prankster now—he even feels responsible for his nephew, which makes Agathe laugh. Frédéric has turned out badly, as they say here. Agathe either doesn't know all about him, or she's not telling. When he left her, everyone very soon found out why, but quite by chance. Alban and I had both left our apartments. It was after July '42. Alban's parents had urged us to do this when they were told Frédéric had joined up. He knew too many things about us; it really was risky. But he didn't denounce anyone. He could have done. Deep down we thought it impossible, but Léandre and Louise were worried about me and the little girl. They too said you never know, and that after all there *was* a war on.

I spent yesterday evening with the children at our place. So that Agathe could go and have dinner with friends. She must start seeing people again so as to make contacts; that's very important for her. She's going to have to bring up her son on her own. Alban came here for the night with Klara. We daren't leave her on her own. Nor does she ask us to. She never asks for anything.

It'll take time. That's our constant theme in the rare moments when Alban and I get to see each other: it'll take time.

We still haven't let Léandre and Louise know yet, nor Antoine and Adeline. Agathe agrees about this. We must wait.

I keep thinking about the first night at home. It was last Thursday, almost a week ago already. I say that, but it feels like an eternity.

I opened the door and went in first. Klara followed, but stopped beside the coat-rack. I said, 'Hang up your coat, Klara, and come in.' I was half-way through the door into

17

the main living-room, but she didn't move. Back to the present tense again. Now she takes a step, and I draw back a little in case she should fall, as I used to do when Victoire was starting to walk. I try to encourage her: 'Come along, Klara, this is the sitting-room.' She lifts one foot. Makes as if to move it further, but then puts it down again beside the other. I am patience personified. For some hours it's been as if I've already accepted and fallen in with her pace. To me, as to her, my surroundings seem unfamiliar. So I just stand there with her. She clutches the handle of the little red case, her closed fist just skin and bones. I don't think anything would make her let go of it. And she's still got the coat which I mistook for a dog bundled up under her right arm. At last she comes into the room, stepping as fastidiously as a cat venturing into a puddle. I burst out laughing, probably because of the tension. 'There aren't any mines here, Klara—it's quite safe to come in!' If it had been Agathe, or the old Klara, I'd have given her a push— put my arms round her, shoved, and then kissed her. But as it is, touching is taboo, and I don't know what to do with my arms.

I go on waiting for her. The inevitable 'Would you like a drink?' is out of place, but I say it anyway. She finally perches on the edge of an armchair. 'Whoops, Klara!' She used to leap, legs flying, into any armchair. 'Whoops! I love armchairs, don't you?' And the boys would say, 'Go on, do it again, Klara! Whoops!'

It brings tears to my eyes to see her now, sitting right on the edge of the chair, as if it might bite her, with her tiny case and her dog—the black coat she hugs as if it were a teddy-bear. There's a lump in my throat, and I don't know what to do.

I sit at her feet on the floor, and she at once slips down on to the carpet, knees bent, leaning back against the chair. She sets her case down carefully and covers it with the coat. I wriggle along on my behind, and lean back against the chair opposite.

I speak gently.

I said: 'We've got a lot of things to tell each other, Klara. How shall we begin? Do *you* want to tell *me* a little? What was it like?'

Her voice was gruff. 'Back there. That's how we refer to it. The name of the place was Oswiecim. They invented another name for it in German. It was a place for saints and beasts. Some became saints. They're all dead. I wouldn't swear to it about any one person in particular, but perhaps . . . perhaps we were all saints. Anyway, we're all dead . . . but if all that is real, you have to suppose the rest of the world was asleep.'

I said: 'I've talked to a few people who got back from Auschwitz, and we found out here, since, that it was one of the most terrible of the camps.'

'I don't know. I was there all the time . . . for months. Twenty-nine, I think. I counted it up . . . twenty-nine. Perhaps you need to come back to see what it's really like. But maybe that's not possible. For six months I've been asking myself that question. But ever since I got out of there, I've known it was a mistake. I'd find it quite natural

19

to go back again. Any time—tomorrow; later on . . . I'd be ready. Even if . . . People would tell me . . . But back there it's as if everything had been like that since the primal darkness—people talk about the primal darkness, but we were *in* it, except for those damned springs and autumns—*they* told us maybe it hadn't existed since time began . . . but it was like some sort of perpetual motion machine—could it ever stop . . . of its own accord? . . . I mean the trains, smoke, trains, smoke and all the misery everywhere . . . We ought not to claim to be human if being human means, implies that—being capable of that . . . what else can you say?'

I'll go on with that evening, that first evening. I must manage to cope with it because of all the difficult things that were said.

Alban arrived. He didn't show any special emotion, but later that night, before we went to sleep, he said to me, 'She's the first person I'm seeing again now that I used to know before. I didn't know any of my other patients in the old days, and that makes a difference. Yes, seeing *her* gave me a shock. At a guess, she must weigh a bit less than forty kilos, but that's not catastrophic. She's been up and about for six months, and I think her vitamins must have done her some good. Have you asked her about her hair? It's odd—it ought to have grown back again by now.'

I went on thinking about it after Alban was asleep.

Although I was tired I couldn't relax, so I thought about Klara's hair. Why wasn't I more shocked about it? Why hadn't I asked myself any questions? I can still see Klara's head, the small head and the short, cropped hair, but a boy's haircut isn't shocking on someone wearing men's clothes. Perhaps if she'd been wearing a dress . . . That must be it— the image of the young man superimposed on the simultaneous knowledge that it was Klara. I must have merged the two together very quickly. Too many things had been happening at once, and I registered the hair automatically, without question. Or, another explanation: Klara's whole appearance was so difficult to take in that her hair was no more perplexing than her clothes, her thinness, her eyes, her whole attitude, and I let the details pass because my main concern was to find the Klara of old, some clue, something tangible to pinch me and tell me I wasn't dreaming. I'd searched mainly for proofs that this was really Klara, but there'd been nothing to reveal the Klara of the past.

Like the good doctor that he is, Alban had had some meat minced and some puréed vegetables prepared. He'd bought soft cheeses, cherry jam, and a cake that wasn't too rich. There were also two bottles of Bordeaux and some pâté de foie.

I rather made fun of this. It's not people's usual idea of a banquet, but Alban said, 'I had to get things that are easy to digest—you never know the state these folk may be in . . .' Well, Klara did eat a little; very little, actually—much less than Victoire would have done. She began by taking some tubes out of her jacket pocket. She had three kinds of vitamin—vitamin C and two sorts of vitamin B. Alban asked to see them and said they'd do, but he'd look into it further—she'd need a special prescription worked out for her. Klara said, 'I've been taking this kind of thing for six months. I ask for them wherever I go, or else I steal them, especially the vitamin C. I've lost five teeth—teeth are an awful problem. In my case it's the big ones at the back, and the others have got holes in them.' Alban said he'd start inquiring into the matter the very next day. He's got friends who are dentists. 'But first and foremost, you're going to have to eat just a little bit more, Klara.' She said, 'I can't—it turns me up.' Alban didn't insist. He said, 'There's plenty of time—your appetite will just come back gradually. But you did quite right to take the vitamins.'

Alban, probably because he's a doctor, took all this more matter-of-factly than I did. I don't know if he saw Klara; or even if he was looking for the real her. To see her just as a patient in the first instance was more practical for him, less painful. That's what I think anyway, though we haven't had time to talk about it.

The dinner was awkward and full of silences, but fortunately full also of Alban's benevolence. Klara ate a spoonful of mashed potato, a tiny piece of meat, a scrape of pâté on a bit of bread, but no cheese or cake or jam. She did drink some wine—two large glasses.

She took some cigarettes out of her pocket—it's incredible, all the stuff she's got in her pockets—and a lighter, a fine silver-plated one, perhaps solid silver. 'I stole it in Prague.' I thought now was the time to bring up the subject of Rainer. I'd been thinking about him all the time.

Alban must have felt he couldn't, or that it was up to me, or that it had already been done.

I (very fast): 'Aren't you going to ask me about Rainer, Klara?'

She: 'He's dead, isn't he?'

I (very fast): 'Yes, in June last year . . . Shot.'

She: 'Who by?'

I: 'In the Saint-Marc maquis, by the Gestapo. Along with some others.'

She: 'Oh, right . . .'

We daren't say any more. She finished her cigarette and lit another. Alban and I accepted a couple from her. We were now sitting riveted to our chairs. Waiting. She said: 'I want to go to America . . . if your brother had still been here, I'd have asked for a divorce. But I'd have gone anyway . . . on my own . . .'

This left us speechless. The words America and divorce were so unreal I scarcely took them in. Alban said nothing. I scraped my cigarette round and round in the ash-tray. What could one say? . . . The phone rang. Alban went and answered it. I sensed some awkwardness. He turned round. 'It's for you, Lika,' he said. 'Victoire wants to say goodnight to you.' Victoire blew lots of kisses into the telephone. I couldn't speak. Finally I mumbled a few platitudes and hung up. Thinking back on it, I believe that was the most difficult moment of all.

Klara smoked away conscientiously and sipped at her wine.

I: 'What if Rainer had come to wait for you at the Lutétia?'

She: 'I don't know. I think I knew he wouldn't be there.'

I: 'But one never knows. Imagine, Klara.'

She: 'I didn't expect him. I didn't expect him to be waiting for me. From what I remember of him, he must deliberately have taken risks . . . So I think I always knew . . . ever since he went south to the Unoccupied Zone to look for an escape route . . . or so he said . . .'

I: 'But he did go and look! Remember how he crossed the dividing line at Châlons several times just to prove it to you, but he couldn't find a way. You can't hold that against him, Klara!'

She: 'All I know is that he looked for heroism, and he found it . . .'

I: 'You're very hard, Klara.'

She: 'No. Every man to his fate. I'm not going to weep for a hero . . . someone granted the blessing of being killed . . . he had good reasons for dying . . . not everyone has such luck . . .'

Perhaps, in her almost flat voice, there was a trace of resentment? I think I heard that, as well as the words.

Thursday, August 2, 1945 Henri-Martin

I'm at home, the children are asleep. We try to share things out equally between Agathe and ourselves. The children like to be together, so that's something. Klara doesn't ask to be left on her own. So we're getting organised. If things go on like this, we've agreed with Agathe to send the children to stay with her parents for a week. We'll have to tell them the real situation then. Agathe says they'll understand, and we needn't worry; Adrien is due to go to Barbery next week, and everything will sort itself out. Adrien will have to be put in the picture too. This makes me sorry for them all. They've been so good to us.

Alban has been and fixed everything at the Lutétia. This evening he's at the rue Richer.

Klara has returned, but not to us.

Klara is back, but she hasn't come back to us.

Another time I tried to talk about Rainer and what happened to him. She said: 'You shut the dead away in a cupboard, lock the door, throw away the key, then forget you've thrown it away, and forget there was ever a cupboard at all.'

No more to be said.

I also asked her about her hair. 'I can't stand hair any more. That's what repelled me most here—the women with their masses of hair, they wear braids wound round their heads, enormous affairs. On the roads there were lots of refugees, fugitives rather, many of them women, and it was the hair that disgusted me straight away. Back there, some women had hair too. It grew again, except in the case of the Jews— theirs was all cut off again. At first, in '42, all I saw was shaven skulls. It was a world without hair, a world that was bald. Imagine that. When I looked closer, I did see some hair. The political prisoners, in their striped uniforms, had some hair after a while—not long hair, but some. The guards, the chief officials and the female Nazis had very well-groomed hair, no doubt by comparison with the others—especially one very young and handsome woman, a horrible bitch with magnificent hair. I found that revolting, perhaps because she was the one with the whip. I cut my own hair. In Berlin I found some clippers, undamaged, in the rubble. After some trouble at first I became quite handy with them, and now I can cut my hair without shaving it off or hurting myself.'

'Have you got the clippers in your case?'

'Yes.'

'But it's so small! A toy suitcase. I used to have one rather like it for my doll's clothes.'

'Yes, so did I.'

'You can't have many things with such a tiny . . .'

'Yes, but whenever I need anything, clothes and so on, I steal it. All I've actually got is the clippers, some panties and other little things, and a toothbrush—all the rest I steal.'

'But now you don't need to steal any more, Klara. It would be silly to get caught.'

'I wouldn't get caught—I'm better at stealing than a gipsy. You yourself have stolen a name, you know your way around . . . it's honest people and fools who die. Back there, what I knew how to do, I forgot, and what I didn't know I learned. The game's up. So I steal. I don't make a very good victim.'

Klara's tranquil arrogance.

Tomorrow I'm going to Barbery with Adrien and the children.

Alban and Agathe are coming on Sunday—I'll go and meet them at Chantilly. All three of us will come back on Monday morning, without the kids. Alban has persuaded Klara to have some more extensive tests at the hospital. She'll see a woman doctor. She won't have a man. The woman's coming to sleep here on Sunday night. Klara interests her, and she's glad to do us this favour. When we told Klara about the arrangement she agreed right away and seemed relieved. We thought she might spend one night in the hospital, but she doesn't want to. A complicated situation, apparently. She can't be alone, but doesn't want to be with anyone else. She needs people near her, but not too near or too many. She said, 'Ever since I was back there, I can't be quite alone any more. All the time I was travelling, I was surrounded by people I didn't know. That doesn't bother me—on the contrary. I've even slept in barns, but there were cattle not far off. Once I was really alone. I don't want to go through that again. I'm not ready.'

I thought it best to go to Barbery with the children. I want to be able to explain and talk about things with Antoine and Adeline. In my opinion we owe them that.

I've found a nice shawl for Adeline, and a little mouth-organ for Antoine—he's lost his. The children are very excited at going to the country. We all need it.

Gradually, Klara has started talking about Auschwitz. Not to me, directly. Alban says she's told him a little, and it was horrible. Doctors carrying out experiments—one of them was called Mendélé or Menkélé—an abominable wretch, anyhow, and not the only one.

Just scraps from time to time, never anything continuous. This evening, in the kitchen with me, she was toying with her food, and out it came, one of those brief revelations that I call scraps, suggesting something else before and after which she won't let us see clearly. There's no continuity in her speech, but she gives the impression that her thoughts run on without pause. The words emerge, you hear them for a moment. I'm reminded of a submarine, there all the time but invisible, until suddenly you see it, then it dives again.

She said: 'It's as if my ghost had stayed on there, together with our thousands of eyes following the smoke, with the wind beating back the smell—thinking of the thousands of eyes that would one day follow our own smoke and our own smell . . . Sometimes I've wondered if I myself wasn't the rising smoke . . . that was at the beginning, when they still burned the bodies in trenches . . . later on . . . but that's what survives . . . the smoke, the smell . . . And to see if I still had an arm, I would touch it, and the same with my legs and feet. You had to test everything, check everything, always. You see, I'm dead, but I don't know how to mourn. I'm like Peter Schlemiel—you remember him: the man who sold his shadow to the devil . . .'

A bit later, while drinking tea and smoking, she said: 'I sometimes wonder if I'm normal. People don't come back from there. My friends were normal. They're dead. I still don't know if I should be glad, or riddled with doubts, I mean at still being here myself. Even if I'm back with sticks instead of arms and legs . . . To have seen one's own skeleton . . . And what an achievement . . . to come back to life after three months, that's better than their Christ, who did it after only three days. But is it possible to come back to life? . . . the body, yes, the body can manage it, but the rest . . .'

That's the first time she's mentioned friends. Will she talk about them again? And how many friends did she have? She didn't say any more about them this evening.

Another scrap:

'One day, a man from one of the working parties told a Czech doctor something that the doctor passed on to me . . . The day before, they'd been put to work on a train that had just arrived . . . and when they opened the doors, no one got out. Imagine . . . twenty-seven days and nights . . . packed in together without anything to eat or drink. The guard of the train was still alive all right. He was still a man. How can one possibly understand . . .'

Later on, still smoking (I smoked a lot too): 'I feel guilty about all those dead people. It's only natural. You don't get over hell.

'A world without words. Do you understand? In that world no words were available. It was another country where people used known words to signify other things, things which couldn't have an exact verbal equivalent in any language. It was a kind of Babel, but I don't think any language ever has or ever will have a vocabulary that could convey it adequately. Even our torturers didn't have a vocabulary for it—they used codes. I know they did.'

As the silence continued, I took the opportunity to talk to her about her jewellery. This afternoon I brought the box back from Trocadéro. It's given us some trouble. No one wanted anything to do with it—neither Alban's parents nor Agathe's, much less Agathe herself. Klara's other things, yes; but not the jewellery. In the end, we kept it ourselves. Alban put it on the top shelf of the cupboard in our room, behind the sheets, where our grandmothers used to hide things. I remember him saying, 'That's it! Stash away the hardware, tell ourselves it's only fake, and think no more about it!'

And certainly we had plenty of other things on our minds afterwards.

31

There are three gold chains, one with big oval links, the other two with olive-shaped links filled in with gold-wire traceries; a magnificent Van Cleef and Arpels bracelet made up of Egyptian cameos and scarabs, with sapphires, rubies and emeralds; two pairs of Lacloche ear-rings, also with cameos decorated with precious stones and outlined with little bars of onyx; and brooches, tie-pins, cuff-links; and rings of all kinds. Her mother had given everything to her daughter, in case she ever needed an additional source of cash.

Klara looked through the things straight away, found a ring, and tried it on. She told me her mother often wore it; she'd inherited it from her own Russian grandmother, Klara's great-grandmother. Of course it wouldn't fit any of Klara's fingers; only—just about—her thumb, where it looked ridiculous. But Klara is obviously keen on it, and put it on the middle finger of her left hand. Perhaps it will stay on if she wedges it with a smaller ring underneath. I said it could probably be made smaller itself, but she said, 'Everything's going to be sold.'

I said: 'You could keep that one—the rest is sure to make quite a lot of money. And there's your apartment in the rue Lafayette. Have you thought of that?'

'You're right—I'd forgotten. They managed to hold on to the apartment.'

'Yes, thanks to Alban's father. He had plenty of contacts. I don't know exactly how he did it, but the place is shut up, and the keys are with the lawyer. Léandre took care of it all, we didn't have any trouble. He'll probably do what's necessary again if you want to sell . . .'

'Yes. You think it's possible?'

'We and Agathe took all the papers and gave them to Léandre. They must be with the lawyer too, I suppose. And as you're the sole owner, there shouldn't be any problem. It may take time, though.'

'How long do you think—?'

'How should I know, Klara? First we need a buyer, and I don't know if people are buying now. I know nothing about business.'

I felt as though I was finding my own Klara again, the Klara of the old days. Just a little, not much as yet, but a little, towards the end. She was almost shy, as if overwhelmed with hope at the thought of selling the apartment. I was reminded of when we went ski-ing, when we were still small. Often, at the top of a slope, she would ask me, almost in a whisper, 'Lika, do you think I can do it?', then immediately, without more ado, take off down the hill as fast as she could. It was difficult for me to catch up with, let alone overtake, her. I was the champion, but she often beat me.

So perhaps, just now, I'd been misled by her timid look. She'd do as she liked anyway.

What I know almost for certain, too, is that she won't reverse her decision to go away and leave Victoire with us.

This evening it was as if there were odd little clues in her voice. Before we separated, she said, 'The train was full of Greeks.'

It's nice to be back here again. It's late. Everyone's asleep. Victoire insisted on sleeping with me. It's so hot she's lying on the bed just in her little panties and vest. A pity Klara can't see her, she's so beautiful, our Victoire. She's grown a lot, but she's still chubby, with a mass of fair curls that's difficult to manage, but so pretty. All the afternoon she and Isidore were shouting and running all over the place, or splashing about in the tin bath that Antoine brought out for them. And by nine o'clock this evening they were fast asleep. Then all the five grown-ups had dinner together. We talked about Klara, of course. I think they were glad I'd come to talk to them and explain her return . . . and the strange decisions she's made.

André was very curious, and asked a lot of questions. I couldn't answer them all. Finally Antoine pointed out Klara hadn't been on a study tour, but André said you heard such a lot of tall stories about the camps that naturally when someone actually came back from them you placed more reliance on what *they* said. Adeline disagreed.

'Do *you* know everything about the Resistance? And yet

you were in it. Klara must know a certain amount about Auschwitz, but maybe not everything if it was such a big place.'

Antoine added: 'In 1914, all *we* knew was our own trench—we didn't even know it was the 1914–1918 war. Nor did the men on the other side, probably. It was only afterwards that we found out!' This made us laugh. It does you good to laugh. And when I'm here I feel like laughing.

Adeline was pleased with the shawl. 'We can be smart young ladies again.' The reputation of Parisian women is quite true: even during the rationing they managed to cope. I must say we and Agathe have coped too. Making room for our and the children's belongings hasn't been a problem. I think Adeline is anxious to get back to Paris; the country gets on her nerves now. Antoine's too. He said this would be the last harvest of 'lawn potatoes'. He's going to have the grass put back this autumn. He played the harmonica for the children this afternoon, and this evening some little pieces by Satie on the piano to calm them down.

It's amazing how Adrien has changed. When we met him in '38 he was sixteen and hadn't reached his full growth. Sometimes he used to come and sleep at his sister's, and joined in our evening parties at Rainer and Klara's. He already had a passion for politics. He liked playing practical jokes with Rainer and Alban. We had wild evenings, with people coming and going all the time on the landing between the two apartments. Klara and I were twenty—born in '18: the children of soldiers wounded or on leave, Papa used to say. Rainer was twenty-six, Alban twenty-five, and Agathe twenty-three. Now we're seven years older, Klara has grey hair, and Rainer would have been thirty-three the day before yesterday. I miss him. Very much. Terribly. My big brother.

When Mother died in September '39, Rainer told me what she'd told him just before we left Berlin. He'd known about her illness right from the start. Mother showed him the results of her tests and told him how the disease was progressing. She was continuing his education, in her own way. It was awful for him, Rainer told me, but she was teaching him both courage and his profession. On the eve of our departure she told him her condition was worsening. The cancer was developing as she'd expected and she'd arranged for what had to be done to end it. He mustn't be angry with her: it would only be when no more than a few months were left. She'd know, and would never let herself be reduced too far by this or any other illness. What mattered most was that Rainer should look after Klara and me as well as he could.

She had kept on a small private practice, just enough to live on. She gave all she had to us, to set ourselves up here or elsewhere. She was very determined about that.

She was still Klara's mother's doctor. She told Rainer, also just before we left, that she'd suggest the necessary way out to Madame Adler too if she wanted it—they'd been even closer friends since Klara and Rainer got married, and that was the best gift she could offer in the circumstances.

When we heard of Madame Adler's death in October '41, Rainer and I thought at first of poison, but we didn't say anything to Klara. What was the point? Anyhow, the news we'd had of the death had been enigmatic, to say the least: two apparently anonymous letters to Rainer, with similar but illegible signatures, one announcing death and the other suicide. Rainer showed only one of the letters to Klara. She worshipped her mother.

At table just now, I described a scene I witnessed at the Lutétia in May.

I'd worked there as a volunteer in April and May. My job was to register people's identities, the names of the places where they'd been detained, their professions etc., and to issue them with information, travel passes to where they were going, and vouchers for cigarettes. And to tell them who was waiting for them, and where, if we knew. And so on. I didn't go in every day, but I was always there waiting when I knew a group was expected; there was always the feeling that 'You never know'. And I wasn't the only one who performed the tiring and irrational chore of coming and waiting in despair. Every day, disappointment; every day I came away saying I'd never go again—it wasn't worth it. But I always did go back, in spite of everything. Meanwhile, there were interesting things to see. It was rather like a lottery. Some people brought photographs; some women were hysterical, others very shy. There were all kinds of people, self-confident ones, pushy ones shoving their way forward. There are always some who trample over others, and some who are trampled over. It's always the same. The new arrivals were silent, disoriented, most of them in poor condition, some on stretchers who were sent straight off to hospital. Alban had some of them as patients at the Salpêtrière. Some died in the following hours or days; those who were in good shape seemed embarrassed: they helped the others and looked neither right nor left.

One evening there were still lots of people around when a new group of travellers arrived. The women showed their photographs as usual. One man left the others to come and confront a woman in the front row.

I was nearby and saw everything.

He said, 'It's me—André.' The woman lowered her arm and the photo, and looked at him blankly. Then he said something extraordinary. 'What's up, Mariette? I tell you it's me, André. Are you deaf?' But he made no move, and neither did she. Just a few seconds of silence, during which you could imagine the story. The little woman battling on all alone for two years, and no longer so ingenuous as to be taken in. She put her hands on her hips and cried, 'Well, I ought to have recognised you—you haven't changed a bit!' Then the other women pushed Mariette forward, and the man was pushed forward by his pals, and there was a murmur of, 'Well, surely they're not going to have a row!' Then there was a little burst of what sounded like forced laughter to encourage them, and the little woman burst into tears in the arms of André, who buried his face in her hair, and then they were alone. Despite everyone's private worries, there was a collective sigh of relief, including one from me. Other couples were reunited that evening too.

'It must be horrible not to be recognised,' Adeline said.

I guessed the man was in his forties, but he may have been under thirty. His wife looked young too.

Beneath André's anger was the anguish of not being recognised, like a cry of pain; but only the anger was visible. Some people don't have a wide range of expressions to choose from, or have lost them, or don't care to use them. In this case it was anger that prevailed. But in such moments of great tension it's easy to pass from the tragic to the comic, from roughness to tenderness.

I can see it again now. It was as if everybody at once felt the couple must be given some help. Yet during those hours of waiting there had been a great deal of loneliness, everyone had his or her own suffering, despair, hope. It wasn't a joyful time, like the Liberation of Paris a year ago. Agathe told me about that. She felt she absolutely must let herself go, together with everyone else; must see the soldiers, hear the shouting, join in with it all. I stayed behind and looked after the children. I was happy for Paris, of course, and for France, but for me the war was not over. There was Rainer and his silence, and the uncertainty about Klara. And the fact that Germany was being pounded to pieces—I couldn't rejoice about that. Agathe had almost lost her voice, shouting, by the time she came home.

'If my brother doesn't come back,' she said, 'I'll never get over it. So it's best if I rejoice now—perhaps it'll be for the last time.'

When we were talking the other day, Klara brought up the name Pazuzu, and this evening I asked the others if they remembered it. Antoine fetched out a box that had all our drawings of Pazuzu in it. It was Adrien who first applied the name to Hitler. Rainer used to talk to us about Babylonian medicine. Mother had given him a kind of encyclopedia of Assyriology, and what he remembered best was Pazuzu the Cruel, the accomplice of storms, who used his wings to spread evil everywhere. 'That's Hitler exactly!' Adrien said. Hence our competition to draw the most horrific picture we could of Pazuzu.

We looked at these efforts this evening. There were portraits of all sorts: Pazuzu grimacing, hideous, black, coloured, with claws, with flippers, with and without a moustache, with long hair, with huge wings. Rainer drew him with wings folded over a tiny penis—'to hide what he hasn't got,' Rainer said. We had produced all kinds of childish fantasies in order to lessen our fears.

This became clear when we looked at them this evening. Our pitiful attempts to free ourselves of our repressed terrors then were like our laughter now at anti-Semitic literature, especially the writings of Céline. Rainer used literally to howl with laughter, saying, 'No German writer is capable of that!', adding, 'except perhaps a German Jew!' Which made us laugh even more, I remember. Only Alban objected to this.

'How beastly,' he said. 'You're turning into anti-Semites yourselves.'

This set us off laughing again, but one day, speaking of Hitler, Klara said, 'The swine! Because of him we're turning into Jews.' But that wasn't the reason for our mirth. (Anyway, can one become a Jew without meaning to? Or rather, these days, can you stop being a Jew if you don't want to?) The fact was that we were instinctively looking for, and finding, the riposte of all the persecuted. Laughter.

It was another way of expressing what Mother used to say so anxiously: 'How stupid can this country get?'

I remember—we talked about it again this evening—we used to recite poems in French, English and Russian (Klara speaks Russian without any accent, as we speak French). Those are our mother tongues. The others reminded me this evening that I used to make them listen to me singing *Deutschland bleiche Mutter* [Germany, pale Mother], and then no one laughed any more. Rainer used to say, 'Lika, you're boring us to death, you and your Brecht!'

Yes, when I think back, how we used to laugh in those days (in spite of those days) about Pazuzu, Céline's pamphlets, and such-like—until Klara went and got herself registered in 1941. Madness. It was as if she'd suddenly converted to Catholicism or Judaism or Nazism—it made no sense. I had no peace after that. I didn't let it show, but I did all I could to get her to move, to go away. She could have lived at my place and I at hers. Agathe made the same suggestion, and so did Antoine and Adeline here at Barbery. It was the least possible precaution, and she wouldn't do anything else; above all she wouldn't change her name, though that too was a possible solution. Rainer looked wildly everywhere; they both wanted to go away. The only thing all three of us agreed about was that they couldn't take refuge with Lisa in Tours. We didn't want to compromise Lisa, who not only had three young children, but also a husband who, as we now know, could not be trusted. Dear Lisa tried to insist, but we were firm. Mother wouldn't have wanted it, either.

I remember Lisa living with us in Berlin, Lisa and her kindly-meant but demanding lessons (dictation, grammar, the fables of La Fontaine, Victor Hugo, Ronsard, Lamartine and so on), her pride at being a native of Tours: 'Pay attention, children, I'm speaking the French of Touraine'— as if she was talking of some rare vintage.

I'm going to have to tell her about Klara and Victoire. She already knows about Rainer.

It was with reference to Berlin that Klara first uttered the name Pazuzu. She said, 'If I hadn't loved the place, I'd have been able to laugh again in Berlin, because right away it made me think of Pazuzu. He'd said you won't recognise Germany any more, so one couldn't help thinking of him in Berlin. The Germans were right to believe him, if you look at Dresden, Berlin, Leipzig, Linz and all the other cities lying in ruins. Hitler wasn't lying—Germany *is* unrecognisable now. But I didn't laugh. If I'd had any tears left, I'd have shed them for Berlin. It wasn't just ordinary wartime bombing, it was a pounding, a rain of bombs meant as a forced expiation. Germany cleansed itself of its Jews by fire, Germany was cleansed of its Nazis by fire.'

I said, 'Do you really believe that?' She said, 'No.'

'I wasn't there during the bombing,' she added. 'I arrived in June, so I might have taken what I saw as a natural catastrophe, not a punishment. I thought it was fate, not chastisement. I wasn't there for the days of fire and destruction. I arrived among the ruins. A time for pity.'

'Pity?' I said.

'Yes, pity.'

Later she said, 'I got some good photos.'

She explained that she'd found—she didn't say stolen—a camera with part of a roll of film left in it. She'd finished the film, removed it, and left the camera behind.

'I was able to take eight shots—the others must have been pictures of nice fat Nazis.'

I wonder what she didn't do in Berlin. She stayed there for three weeks, she told me.

Monday, August 6, 1945 Henri-Martin

I'm in the sitting-room at home.

Klara's in our room. Asleep. It's ten o'clock. I go and check every quarter of an hour, but she's always asleep. She hasn't moved. Alban just phoned and told me not to worry.

Anyhow, a funny thing happened this afternoon. We'll call it tragi-comic if, as Alban insists, nothing serious is likely to come of it.

We both came back from Barbery this morning. Agathe's staying on till Wednesday. I think they wanted to discuss her professional future. Agathe herself would like to go into fashion design, but her father can help her in interior decorating, a field where he has a lot of useful contacts. Antoine thinks she'd stand a very good chance in that line because of her training and qualifications.

I wanted to have today to myself, to tidy up the house a bit and top up our provisions—I've still got some ration cards left. It was arranged that I'm to go back to the rue Richer this evening to sleep. So first I went round the shops. I got back to hear the phone ringing, so I dumped all my things in the hall. It was Alban, to say he was bringing Klara home; something had happened, though it wasn't serious. At this I let out a cry, but he said, 'It's nothing, Lika, nothing. She's asleep—we'll put her in our room.' I could hear he was almost laughing, but I couldn't make out what was going on and was very worried. However, he hung up and left me still in the dark. I don't know for how long—long enough for me to imagine all kinds of crazy things. I left the door ajar and waited for them.

Their arrival gave me a shock. Alban was still in his long white doctor's coat, carrying Klara in his arms. He called to me from the door, 'Don't worry, Lika—she's only sleeping, as I said.' His tone of voice was strange, and it was strange, too, to hear him say that with Klara lying in his arms as if she were dead. Fortunately I was rooted to the spot. I didn't even follow him into the bedroom.

In the sitting-room Alban slumped into a chair, smiling broadly.

'Talk about a bag of bones!' he said. 'Let's have a coffee, Lika, and I'll explain. After that I must go back . . . Don't be silly. If it was serious I wouldn't have brought her here. The hospital isn't a dormitory, and I keep telling you she's only sleeping. She's asleep, that's all. Asleep!'

He seems quite unworried, and that reassures me.

So I'm trying to reconstruct what happened. If I've got it right, Alban got a phone call from a café in the rue de Buci. He arranged for a colleague to replace him. Everyone in his department has known about Klara's case from the start. So he rushed off as fast as he could. The people in the café were waiting for him when he arrived in his white coat and with what he calls his paraphernalia. They'd laid Klara down on an upholstered bench at the back of the café. At first Alban thought, like the others, that she'd fainted. He took her pulse, listened to her heart through his stethoscope, and then apparently realised she was fast asleep. Her pulse was regular, she was breathing freely, she was just somebody perfectly normal who'd fallen asleep. He even managed to take her blood pressure in her upper arm. She offered no resistance—just pulled a face, Alban said. Her blood pressure was low, but not alarmingly so. When he told the people in the café what he thought, they were astonished. Then they told him what they knew.

Klara had been sitting for some time at a table at the front of the café near the windows. Then a customer came in, saw Klara, walked over to her and probably said something—the other people couldn't be sure; they weren't paying attention. It was only when she stood up and gave him a resounding slap in the face that they began to take notice. She hit him as hard as she could, they told Alban: 'She's such a little thing, all skin and bones, but you should have seen the other one pouring with blood—the great oaf didn't even defend himself!' And the manageress said, 'When we realised what had happened, I rushed over. Her sleeve was turned back, and I saw the numbers. We'd heard about the tattoos, but no one had ever seen them with their own eyes.'

Alban gave a good imitation of the manageress, and couldn't help laughing.

He explained that the man had attacked Klara because he took her for a '*tondue*', one of the Frenchwomen who'd had their hair shaved off last year to punish them for being too friendly with the Germans during the war. I don't know if Klara is even aware of those deplorable happenings. Anyway, there was no need to hold her back after she hit the man. According to the people in the café, she fell down straight away on to the table, then on to the floor. Alban thinks she must have lost consciousness for a while, perhaps come to when they moved her, then suddenly fell asleep.

I asked if the man might lodge a complaint, but according to the witnesses' account he looked ashamed—he must have seen the tattooed numbers too. He cleaned himself up and left, saying he'd be back some time; so no problem there. Alban said, 'What an ass! Imagining you'd see any *tondues* now! A year later! Anyway, he took our phone numbers so that he could find out how our little boxer gets on!'

I wondered how they'd found Alban's phone number in the first place. He said he'd made Klara keep it and our home number on a visiting card in her pocket. On the card he'd written, 'In case of emergency, please get in touch at once with Dr Naël,' adding the name and number of his department at the hospital. Klara's supposed to have agreed to this arrangement. Perhaps, when she fell down, everything dropped out of her pocket, together with the keys. Or perhaps the people searched her.

This shows me Alban isn't as easy in his mind as he tries to seem, and that he has his reasons. We'll have the results of the tests on Wednesday.

He also said he'd tell me about the meeting between Klara and Fabienne. Fabienne hasn't managed to give her a complete examination. Klara refused to take any clothes off below the waist, so we know she weighs thirty-eight kilos in her trousers and climbing boots, which isn't much for someone over five feet tall. Even if their first encounter wasn't easy, Alban said, Fabienne is very struck with her. Alban's pleased because he thinks this colleague of his is the right person for Klara. She's tactful, and cheerful as well as firm. If Klara agrees, Fabienne can be our medical go-between. She's already persuaded her to drink milk with sugar in it!

On Sunday evening at Barbery, Alban saw my notebook on the table in our room. He asked what it was, then if he could read it. I'm quite willing to let him. It's just notes, so I don't mind. Then he said something very funny.

'I didn't know a journal had so much dialogue in it. It's like a story—it makes me want to know what happens next.'

Frankly, I don't know how you're supposed to write a journal, or even if there *is* a special way of doing it. The dialogue in mine is there for a practical reason—to help me get on faster. I try to be as accurate as possible in reconstructing thoughts while they're in the process of being spoken. I reproduce what I can or what I choose to. But how do you tell the difference between wanting to do something and being able to?

It's midday, and they're both still asleep. I daren't make any noise. I heard Alban come home. He came into the bedroom, looked at Klara with a torch, and just stroked my hair a little. He must be either in the back bedroom or in Victoire's room. I lay down on the bed beside Klara at about three in the morning. A little while ago she'd turned and was lying on her side. By now she must have been asleep for eighteen hours. I hope it's all right.

Alban also told me what happened when he explained Klara's situation to the people in the café. Perhaps because of all the tension since she got back, or the fright we'd had over the phone call, or maybe because we'd been through several exhausting years already, anyhow he couldn't help laughing. He was very embarrassed, and tried to explain that Klara had had practically no sleep for a fortnight, and we ourselves hadn't had much either, and then there she was, all of a sudden, sleeping like a baby—it was too comical, especially after what she'd done to the man in the café. He got a stomach-ache, trying to stop himself laughing. It suddenly struck him that after Klara's outburst, the people in the café might think he was mad too and be suspicious, might even wonder if he really was a doctor. These apprehensions helped him to sober down, but it was still difficult.

I know without being told that Alban didn't like the way he'd burst out laughing. Perhaps he's worried about it.

We talked about Victoire on the way back from Barbery yesterday. On Sunday she was difficult and wore us all out. I'd taken the children with me to meet Agathe and Alban at the station, whereupon she kept wanting to sit on Alban's knee and trying to make him play with her. We had to scold her twice at table. She makes a row until someone pays attention, then clams up and just rushes about all over the place.

In the afternoon we sat under the lime tree. Adrien had managed to persuade Victoire to play with Isidore, to get them away from the table. Messing about with the watering-can held Victoire's attention for a while, but she soon came back to us. By tacit agreement we don't talk about Klara in front of her. We can't, anyway. It's difficult to have an uninterrupted conversation. Only at dinner did we get some peace, but before that, Victoire made a fuss about wanting to sleep in our bed. Agathe and Alban were firm. Agathe said, 'Malika and Palan are sweethearts this evening, so you're going to sleep in my room.' But Victoire wanted to be sweethearts with us, and Isidore said in the loud voice that always makes us laugh, 'I'm going to be sweethearts too.' I admit it upsets me terribly to scold Victoire, but we can't just let her go on like this. You can tell she's unhappy from her nervous laugh; she shouts more than usual and is inclined to whine. While we were giving both children dinner in the kitchen, she said defiantly, 'Isidore's my little brother, not yours'. She was very serious. But he's wily enough too, and said in the same tone of voice, 'Yes, and Victoire's my little sister, not yours.' Up till now, he's managed remarkably well not to be completely swallowed up by her. When she tries to lord it over him, he disarms her by going along with it. She once said, 'Victoire isn't nasty,' which shows she's not at ease with herself. Someone answered, 'No, you're not nasty, but you are grumpy.' She can live with that; it's not so serious.

It's true she doesn't see us much together any more. Sunday was the first time since Klara came back. Quite simply, she's anxious.

We must find an explanation she can understand. We should also get around to a proper discussion with Klara herself to find out exactly what she wants. Alban thinks it's too soon yet. So do I.

Klara slept for twenty-two or twenty-three hours running. She woke at about three on Tuesday afternoon. I was in the room just then, looking for some things in the chest of drawers. I didn't turn round—I could see everything in the mirror. Perhaps it was the sound of the drawer that woke her up.

She rolled over on her back, her eyes shut. 'Klara, Klara,' I said very softly. She drew up her knees, then stretched out again with her arms up on the pillow. I could see her tattoo clearly for the first time. Her eyes were still closed; I didn't move, but waited until she said, *'Ich bin hungrig.'* ['I'm hungry'] Then I turned to her again: 'Are you asleep, Klara?' She said yes, and again, *'Ich bin hungrig.'* I sat down at the other side of the bed; she still kept her eyes shut.

'Are you asleep?' I looked more closely at her tattoo; I had a lump in my throat. It's so frightful. The force of it really struck me there, close to her as she was waking up. She smelled strongly of sweat . . . she'd opened her eyes a moment, then closed them again. I didn't feel I could touch her. I'd have liked to put on some music to give her a pleasant awakening, but instead I just hummed something softly. I could see she was listening, so I said, 'Are you hungry, Klara?' She said, 'I spoke German.' 'Yes, just a little,' I answered. 'I must forget it,' she said. 'Yes, I am a bit hungry.'

'What would you like?'

'Some *café au lait* and some bread and butter.'

'That's fine, Klara! Would you like to go to the bathroom first?'

'Yes, a bath.'

'I hope there'll be enough hot water left—Alban's just had a shower.'

'It doesn't matter.'

I told Alban, who'd by now emerged from the shower, and we ran a bath—it was only tepid, so I put a big bowl of water on to boil, which we could add to heat the bath up.

Klara didn't appear until at least half an hour later. We'd got everything ready. Fortunately, Adeline had given me some butter and three jars of plum jam. Klara came in carrying her shoes in her hand, which looked rather comical. She had what was probably meant to be a smile on her face, but finally it turned into a grimace, and there was a strange gurgle in her voice when she said, with a German accent, 'I'ff bin asleep, the old hag needed it'. Perhaps the odd sound was laughter, but if so it was a kind of laughter never heard before, as if it issued from a larynx which only remembered what laughter was.

I offered her some clean clothes, but she said all she wanted was some panties, some socks and a pullover.

She declined my trousers—she wanted to keep her own.

We heard the sound of the bathroom door being bolted, and Alban called out, 'Klara, we won't come in, but I'd rather you didn't bolt the door, if you don't mind.'

Silence, then Alban heard her say, 'Shit!'

She didn't unbolt the door.

I remembered her telling me how embarrassing it was for the women during the first days in the camps—and how they struggled to keep the door shut when they went to the lavatory.

A bit later on, I went and told her to help herself to my perfume if she wished.

Silence, then, aggressively: 'Why, do I smell?'

I was suddenly rather annoyed, and said, 'Yes, Klara, you do smell, actually, but please yourself!'

Alban said, 'Calm down, Lika!', then, as if to persuade himself, 'We must all keep calm . . .'

While we were waiting for Klara in the kitchen, Alban told me something about the examination with Fabienne. After a rough check of Klara's weight, Fabienne exclaimed, 'This is impossible! You really must eat, Klara! There's nothing to stop you, and if you don't, you won't survive. And besides, you're young, and it isn't pretty to be so thin— a few curves would be a great improvement!'

Alban said, 'Fabienne doesn't beat about the bush, but maybe that's not a bad thing, and she's the sort of person who can get away with it.'

Apparently Klara said, 'What do you know about it, you big fat cow?' I made Alban say that again. It was true—she'd called Fabienne a big fat cow. Fabienne, it seems, burst out laughing. Alban told me his colleague is a short woman in her forties and not at all fat. Actually, according to Fabienne herself, the two women quite took to each other, hence the hot milk that Klara agreed to drink at night. Fabienne was still laughing when she told Alban about what had happened. Thinking it over, she wondered if what Klara had called her mightn't be a compliment in some kind of vocabulary peculiar to the camps.

Moreover, Klara hadn't menstruated since she was in the transit camp at Drancy—that is, since 1942—but in fact she hadn't had a period since before Victoire was conceived, except one, a month after the birth. As far as this was concerned, Alban wasn't telling me anything I didn't know: Klara had told me about it already, in her own way.

'At least they won't have had that much of our blood in the camps,' she said. She airily went on to explain how practical it was not to have to deal with her normal cycle there, where there was already dysentery and other horrors to cope with—things so awful and incredible I find it hard to write about them.

'The French called it *chiasse*—the trots. A good word, that—*chiasse*.

'(The German *Bauchfluss* isn't bad either—belly-flux.) It was everywhere, and we had no water to wash with, and no clean clothes to change into. Those Nazis are a filthy lot. They can't feel clean unless others are dirty. And no one can be clean in those circumstances. Even animals can't bear it—they lick themselves. As we might have done too. But imagine—with blood over everything as well—no, we did the best we could.'

We had dinner with Klara sitting there quite imperturbable and with her hair still wet. She had put on some perfume—some of Alban's . . .

He said: 'My word, Klarinette—you certainly had a good snooze while you were at it!'

Klara: 'How long?'

I: 'Twenty-two or twenty-three hours—it depends when you started.'

Klara: 'Yes, and without any nightmares. How did I get back here from the café?'

Alban: 'With me, Klara.'

We soon gave up our previous banter. Alban had to drop his Klarinette!

I asked: 'Are we allowed to know what happened? Do you remember?'

Klara: 'Yes. Just now it all came back to me. Some tall chap came over to my table and said, "Well, doll, had some fun, did you?" He tried to touch my head. I sort of saw red, and hit him, with my fist and with the ring. I drew blood— I saw that. But I don't remember anything afterwards . . .'

I: 'You didn't just slap his face, then—you punched him?'

She: 'Yes, with my fist. But I've lost the ring.'

Alban rushed into the bathroom and came back with the ring. He'd left it in the pocket of his trousers, in the dirty linen basket.

Klara put it on again. It's the square one, set with six little pointed diamonds. Easy to believe it drew blood! I don't find it pretty, but it's certainly efficient!

I: 'And do you feel better now? A long sleep always does you good, doesn't it?'

She: 'Yes, but I hurt all over.'

Alban: 'That's only to be expected, after lying without moving for more than twenty hours. And you haven't enough flesh on your bones to act as a cushion, so naturally you feel it now. You'll feel better tomorrow.'

There was no more to be said about the rue de Buci incident. We changed the subject.

Alban: 'So your meeting with Fabienne went off all right?'

She: 'She told you about it.'

Alban: 'Yes, a bit . . . so you call my friend a big fat cow?'

She gave her strange laugh again, like when she came out of the bedroom with her shoes in her hand.

Klara: 'She'd have made a good *blockova* back there in the camps.'

We must have looked puzzled.

Klara: 'In Polish that means the woman in charge of a female block of prisoners—the chief. My friend from Prague was a *blockova*, a good one, like your friend. A good chief is rare. My friend from Prague was like your colleague.'

I: 'Where is she now?'

She: 'Dead.'

~

Silence.

I: 'What about your other friends? You told me the other day you had several . . .'

She: 'Three. I had three friends. The one from Prague, who was a photographer like me. The one from Linz, the youngest, a law student. And the one from Cracow, a nurse —no, not a nurse, she helped children to be born.'

Alban: 'A midwife.'

She: 'Yes, a midwife. She killed several children.'

We fell silent. Alban started to fidget on his chair, and rubbed his eyes with the flat of his hands.

Klara: 'She gave them injections when she could; otherwise, she strangled them . . . to save the mother . . . No one ever came back from there with a baby. So my Polish friend did that. She always tried to kill herself afterwards; tried to throw herself on to the barbed wire. But it was typhus that killed her. In the winter of '44.'

We were silent again. Later:

'What about the one from Linz?' I asked.

'The little one, the youngest, she was only twenty. She died in the winter of '44 too. It was the typhus that killed her as well. The typhus and I.'

We were still silent, just looking at her.

Klara: 'I killed several people. One was a bitch, a horrible bitch. That was an accident. We arranged a very good accident . . .'

She gave that gurgling laugh again.

I: '*You* killed her?'

'I helped. Several of us did it, for a lark. We laughed all the time we were at it—a good joke. I killed several times— that time happily and as one of a team, and another time on my own and full of grief . . . the girl from Linz . . . It was only a question of days or even hours . . . she'd asked me to do it . . . implored . . . I'd promised . . . I had no choice about *how* to do it.'

Silence from us. Then, because one had to go through with it:

Alban: 'How?'

Klara, putting her hands round her neck: 'Strangled.'

It was her turn to look at us, and probably we looked stupid or frightened, I don't know. All I do know is that there I sat, not thinking of anything, not daring to think. Her great eyes gazed at us, grey, grey-blue, tranquil and cold.

She gave her harsh, ersatz laugh again.

'You should see your faces,' she said, and then almost

lightly, with a sigh, 'You can't imagine how long it takes a skeleton to die.'

We were silent again, waiting. We both sensed she wanted to go on. She realised we were ready to listen. We had to. We had to hear all she wanted to say. She took her time.

Klara: 'I have no tears left to tell you that my three friends didn't last out, my normal friends . . . all three of them are dead, I lost all three of them in the winter of '44, the beginning of '44, February, I think. I did all I could to save them all, one after the other, I wore myself out . . . I stole, lied, fought, physically fought, took risks—exactly as you would have done, Lika, as you both would have done, as they would have done themselves—mad things, ridiculous things, but in those circumstances they were crazy, provocative—I'm not boasting . . .

'Later on, no. Later on, I was helped too. I went on helping, but I wasn't generous any more, not enough, never enough any more . . . I was careful, I calculated what I did for people, yes, I might as well admit it, because above all I didn't want any more friends, I refused, refused more and more often . . . everything I did was calculated, in order to help me last out; I measured out the help I gave according to what it would get me in return, I even learned to plan ahead, as in a game of chess. But in the end, no, I was too worn out, your mind gets like cotton-wool . . . how shall I put it—it's all a fog, and so chance and luck no longer matter. That's all. Nothing noble about it. In fact, nothing was ever noble for me after my friends died. Just the task to be carried out every day in order to last out. In another life you'd call it ignominious, but I don't feel any remorse about that, just as I hadn't felt any scruples before. I just carried on with the little bit of intelligence I had left, and the wariness of a brute beast, that's all.'

Silence from us again. Later:

I: 'What were their names?'
    She: '?'
I: 'Their first names . . . your friends . . .'
    She: 'All three had pretty names.'
We realised nothing would have made her utter their names.
    I: 'You don't want to tell us, is that it?'
    She: 'Yes, that's right. They haven't any graves. When I die, their names will die. I wandered about Europe partly for them. I went to Cracow and Prague and Linz for them—and all over Germany on my own account—I was just as dead myself . . . I was supposed to be a survivor. *Sous*vivor* would be more like it. People ought to be more careful with words. I looked up at the sky over Cracow, over Prague, and over Linz, thinking of them. I conducted three funerals all on my own . . . the memory of them in my mind was their coffin. Their names are in me and I am their gravestone . . . So now you know.'

~

*[*Tr.* A pun on the French 'sur' = over, and 'sous' = under.]

61

All these pages have been difficult to write. What it must have been like to live through . . .

But because she has done and experienced and suffered all this, we owe it to her to listen to her, and to understand if we can. That's what she wants. She probably doesn't understand the violence she's doing us. Unless she sees it all as necessary to her own equilibrium in the future. She's probably acquired a sound instinct about what she has to do to last out, as she puts it, in any circumstances.

Afterwards we went to the Champ-de-Mars for a breath of air. Alban and I were exhausted. In the evening we drove her back to the rue Richer. She'd assured us she could be on her own that night and wouldn't sleep. We made her promise to take a taxi back to our place if anything went wrong. But everything was all right, and Alban and I were able to have the evening to ourselves. We talked a lot. He told me about Japan, and how they'd dropped an atomic bomb on a city there on Monday, killing thousands of people in a few seconds. Horrible. I ought to listen to the radio more.

The city was Irochima. The day before yesterday they dropped an atomic bomb on Nagasaki—there's no end to it. Hundreds of thousands killed in both cities—civilians, naturally. In just a few seconds. Japan would have surrendered anyway, so why, why more deaths? And no one knows anything about the consequences. Just now, on the phone, Alban told me how horrified he is. No one knows what the ultimate effects will be for the living, or even, he said, for children as yet unborn whose parents might have been affected. And for how many years or decades will all that last?

I went back to the café to thank them for their kindness. I told them Klara had slept for twenty hours on end. The woman there kept saying, 'Incredible, incredible! Poor young lady.' I gave them one of the jars of plum jam Adeline had given me. They were very pleased to have it.

While I was at the bar, the waiter went over to a customer sitting at a table near the window. He said something to him and brought him back to the bar. It was Klara's punch-ball.

'I'm Jérôme Legris, the guilty party,' he said, 'I don't know what to do. You must be a friend of the young lady's.'

I felt like laughing, because he had a black eye, and I actually did laugh when I said that Klara certainly hadn't done things by halves. That lightened the atmosphere.

'She did some damage, I see,' I added.

'Oh, nothing serious,' he answered, 'and I asked for it . . . She's gone a bit funny, hasn't she?'

I said, 'Yes and no—or rather, no. She has her reasons. We shouldn't jump to conclusions—after twenty-nine months in the camps, it's hard to tell.'

They all seemed to agree, and to be really moved by what I'd told them.

'You live and learn,' said the manager of the café. 'I'd never have believed it. We've seen some funny things here, but never a little skeleton in a fury like that!'

The phrase 'little skeleton' seemed to appeal to them. It wasn't said maliciously—rather, with a touch of admiration and amusement. It seemed to me they were all as foolish as Monsieur Legris himself, and on seeing Klara had all supposed she was one of the *tondues*, and were now exaggerating their sympathy perhaps to try to make up for their error. This impression was reinforced when the waiter said to the young man, 'Right, you spoke out of turn, but it could have happened to any of us. How were you to know?' But the young man stuck to his guns, saying, 'Yes, but I was

64

the one who opened my big mouth, so naturally I was the one who had to pay for it.'

I thought he was overdoing it, and said, 'Right, but Klara's not dead—the dust-up even did her good—because of it she was able to sleep for twenty-two hours. Anyway, what you said wasn't very clever even if she had been a *tondue*. It was horrible, what they did to the women here. I'm against it, let me tell you, and I think we'd better change the subject, because *I'm* not a little skeleton . . .'

Then they all said yes, let's drop it, it's not worth it, everyone has the right to an opinion, we're not going to fight over this, we've had enough fighting these last five years.

Before the young man came to the bar, the manageress had said, as if to excuse him, that he'd been in the S.T.O. (Service du Travail Obligatoire)—one of the French workers deported to Germany to help with the German war effort—and that his fiancée had jilted him when he came home. According to her, that would account for his thoughtless attack on Klara.

But perhaps he'd volunteered to go to Germany. Liars like that are all the more vindictive for having been cowards themselves.

I feel relieved, as if what I've just done has freed me of some fear, something I dreaded, I didn't know exactly what. I know now. It had been there from the first: if she hadn't punched that man, she'd have hit me.

The city in Japan that was bombed is spelt Hiroshima.

Yesterday we and Agathe went to lunch at Barbery.

The children are going to stay there for another fortnight. Adrien looks after them. They're both in great form. Victoire's not so temperamental now; she was very sweet right up to when we left, and then she didn't ask to come back with us. Of course, Barbery is a miniature Paradise for children.

Agathe hadn't mentioned it to me, but Antoine asked us if it would be possible for him to buy back Klara's apartment for Agathe. Her own apartment is not for sale, but she could use one place or the other for her professional activity, as a sort of architect's office. It would be a good thing if Antoine and Léandre were to meet at the notary's and make Klara some offers. Alban has phoned his father about it. Léandre is quite happy to see to everything, including finding the financing for Antoine, who'll have to sell a farm to buy the apartment.

Klara said everything was all right by her. With the jewellery she'd already be quite well off, and her own place could be sold quite cheap; she wouldn't need much money.

I don't think she really knows exactly how much she needs. Anyhow, it doesn't matter, there's no great problem about that side of things. For the moment, we take care of her expenses, and that's fine. Anyway, she doesn't want anything out of the ordinary. She won't buy any clothes. And all she's accepted as a gift is two pairs of my climbing pants, altered to fit her by Agathe, according to measurements supplied by me. The waist had to be taken in a lot. She always dresses warmly, with socks and her big boots. But she often feels cold, though the summer heat is sometimes too much for the rest of us.

We're getting used to the way she looks. Her hair's beginning to grow again a little. She hasn't cut it again yet, but there's no curl in it now; it's just short and straight.

I finally told Klara I was writing in order to try to get things straight in my mind. I was curious to know how she'd react. I'd imagined every possible kind of response. But I was surprised to get the impression that she was interested, and this encouraged me to ask her if she'd read over some passages occasionally to check that I'd set down correctly what she'd said or meant. She said we could try. Perhaps I'd been a bit too hasty, for afterwards I found I didn't care for the idea any more.

This evening she said, 'Luckily for me I was almost always angry. Always or almost always, and at the critical moment I always felt the kind of shock that produces quick reactions.

Some people are born to say yes, and others are born to say no.'

Stupidly, I said, 'You said yes to life.'

'I didn't say yes, I said no to everything. Perhaps it was a yes, as you say, but I thought of it as a no—that was probably what suited me best. If it had been a yes I'd be dead, physically dead. I always said no. Only angels say yes—angels and fools.'

'But you deliberately got caught—you could have avoided it.'

'True, and that cured me of any yeses in the future. Ever since, I've never thought yes. But even if negatives are also in a way affirmatives, it still changes everything if you think of yeses as nos.'

'Why did you go and register?'

'I didn't do it because I wanted to be deported. I did it out of loyalty to my mother. I didn't even think about the laws or what was actually happening. I did it for just one reason—to be close to my dead mother. To do what she would have done: she was law-abiding to a fault, and so was I. I didn't see it as entailing my own death. Who can believe in his or her own death at the age of twenty-three? Did you?'

'Yes, I've always believed in death, in the possibility of my own death, just the possibility, even if, as you say, one doesn't really believe it.'

'So you *did* believe in it.'

'Yes. Otherwise, why should I have taken another name and got forged papers?'

'You believed in death, and I didn't, couldn't. That

probably accounts for the only differences between us . . .'

'I don't know.'

'To tell the truth, I can't prove it was because of my mother—that's something I say to give a reason for an act that hasn't got one; a false reason is still a reason. But perhaps there are acts without reason, without any reason at all. Do there have to be reasons? Does a stupid act have reasons, one reason, a set of reasons? If there are reasons for everything, we have to find the reasons for the horror people experienced in the camps. We must find them, otherwise how can we demand reasons for the absurd acts of every individual? If no one can give the whys and wherefores of the camps, everyone is justified in all his acts, even the most bloodthirsty. If no one can give the answer, the world is doomed.'

'Do you think we'll find the reasons? Because there's more than one. It's impossible.'

'I still don't understand what happened to me, nor why, nor even how. The big why belongs to others; the how, or the little why, I'm partly responsible for them—as you say, my stupidity in getting caught like that—that multiplied by the number of others who did the same, that's the first question, one I may be able to answer some day; but the overall why, the overall answer, that's for the historians. But for each of the people arrested and killed, there's no individual cause in itself. None. And overall answers don't interest me. I've been humiliated enough as just one fish in the shoal, so I dodge that question. Henceforth I only want to be the one fish in the net, and to know how and why I got there. I want to know all I can about the whys and wherefores in my own life, not depend any more on the madness of a corporal, the idiocy of a people, or any of the words like Flag, Nation, War and History. Never again. Now I shall escape in time.'

Later on, Klara kept dwelling on her astonishment, still as great as ever, at what she'd experienced. I can report only roughly what she said.

'The number of ordinary people, that's what struck me, ordinary people, I mean the whole world of people who never go to prison, such as children, obviously; old people who never go to prison, little old couples; mothers with a child or children; quiet men. I remember thinking right away—I was still at the beginning—the rogues have put all the respectable people in prison. I've never seen so many ordinary people—it was like when the streets are crowded in the evenings near Christmas—ordinary people you don't know; if you did they wouldn't be ordinary. If I'd known each one, none would have been ordinary, and everyone could have said that. No one could remember such a great misfortune, such great cruelty, such total cruelty; no one had ever heard or read of anything approaching it, so everyone behaved ordinarily. The only difference was that everything was a bit more intensely what it was—it was a matter of degree, but within the bounds of ordinariness. In this story, only the tormentors were extraordinary—not those in the administration, but the minor staff, the riff-raff.

But we ourselves, no, quite ordinary, with ordinary pre-occupations, and even those whose preoccupations weren't ordinary became like the rest, with ordinary preoccupations. And perhaps that was what was most extraordinary about that life—everyone became preoccupied only with bread, water, shoes, warm clothes, a little sleep, nothing else. All our references were to something below or beside the reality. In any case, nothing was of any help in that life except oneself, standing up to things all alone, dying all alone.'

'Everyone dies all alone.'

'Yes, but there it was more alone because of the abjection . . . you don't know what that is . . .'

Silence . . . a long silence . . .

'I didn't learn anything at Oswiecim except that I'm stronger than I'd have thought.'

'That's a lot.'

'I could have learned it some other way; what happened to me wasn't indispensable. You don't have to learn everything the hard way . . .'

'After we ordinary people had been "selected for elimination" from among the rest of the prisoners, the nature of each of us became more marked. One was more this, more that. In the camps, you're more cowardly, more spineless, more dynamic, more stupid, more passive, more charitable, more grasping, more inventive, stronger, or weaker. It's the realm of negation or intensification.'

'And you—what were you?'

'More everything, according to the day, the state I was in, the weather—like everyone else. For me it was negation or intensification, just the same as for everyone else.'

'Did you always think?'

'Less and less as time went by. Some people went mad. Sometimes you have to be just a body. When I could, I was glad to think again, to get the machine going again, though it was difficult and strange. And sometimes—you won't believe me—but I refused to think, it disgusted, yes, disgusted me, as if I couldn't trust myself, as if it was dangerous. You just had to keep the machinery going, the minimum necessary for coping with all the unthinkable things that might happen in a day, an hour, a moment. Just the basics. I've made up for it since. I never stop thinking now. I may not think properly, and I'm not sure it really is thought . . . it's like it, but no, I don't believe I think yet— no, my thoughts aren't yet thought. I don't know what to call them.'

14/8 Tuesday

I arrange things so that Klara talks to me every day about what it was like at Auschwitz. She responds quite willingly, sometimes at length, sometimes briefly. At first I often have to ask her; she doesn't always begin of her own accord. She chooses different aspects for Alban and me. We probably ask her different questions too.

This afternoon I asked her if she ever laughed.

'Yes, at first. But there was a last time. I remember that. After I arrived, from August to November '42, I was in a tough working-party. Very tough. Shifting earth; navvies' work. It was there I made friends with the girl from Prague. The girl from Linz was later, and then, in November, the friend from Cracow.

'The first two weeks, we managed to laugh. We were still in fairly good form, our strength hadn't been too over-taxed, and we laughed to ward off depression, and both of us were beside ourselves with anger. Perhaps that was what first brought us together—the same state of mind. Then, very soon, fatigue and fading strength brought cynicism and

73

a kind of cruel humour—not towards ourselves, towards others. Not against them, but—how can I describe it?—a refusal to feel sorry for them or spare their feelings. We told new arrivals straight away what the camp was like, without offering any consolation or concern; this didn't stop us from helping them, but we were still cruel enough to tell them the truth.

'One day, yes, it was at the beginning, a Polish woman said, "You're lucky to have lived in France—here we used to say, 'happy as God in France'". I said, "God got rounded up in France, he's here in Oswiecim, he goes up in smoke every day, as we're the first to know." We laughed. We laughed for days. We said, "Serve him right—what an idea, to go to France—even God got caught there, and this time he won't escape, he won't be able to collect up his bones. No more resurrection for God . . ." To newcomers who asked what the smell was, we said, "It's God burning, he got himself rounded up in France." They said, "What a stench!" and we said, "Yes, yes, when God burns, he stinks too." It was a kind of consolation to tell oneself that God himself was burning. We weren't trying to say anything philosophical or metaphysical or religious—no, it was just an amusing idea, a joke that kept us going for a few days till something else turned up. We, the people without belief, were the most naked, but not the most helpless, because we had no illusions, and therefore no resentment, just enough rebelliousness not to be resigned, just enough reflexes not to die, to let ourselves die . . . Moses didn't come, nor his brother the lawyer. No Moses, no lawyer. God was an Austrian corporal.

'No one is prepared for the exception to be the rule. There in the camps, all the time, everything—the body, the spirit, what was left of the spirit—expected an accident to happen, what for want of another word might be called an accident—anyhow some horror, something irreparable: even if you actually survived it, it did incurable damage to both body and mind. So you made yourself small; did or didn't do things just in order to last out. We were made cowardly or brave—made to be all the things you can think of, in the passive, so as to live in the passive, outside oneself, in a world where courage and cowardice served the same purpose, where even endurance became ignominy if by any chance you still had a spark of lucidity left to let you see things straight.

'Ignominy . . . you see, it's like those big books we both used to devour, you remember. We both read to our hearts' content in those days, and used to wonder why the author didn't kill his characters off on page twenty—their lives were so awful—unless it was for the pleasure of making them agonise throughout the whole story, and because he took pride in having them hold out for four hundred pages. Well, I was that author, except that the character was myself. I lasted for pages and pages, and I don't know why I didn't let myself die on the twentieth day, except that I too took pride in getting through to the end of that vast novel, one of the worst ever written, with all the sensational twists and turns of a bad novel, with the same absurdity, the same paltriness, the same stupidity.'

'But in that world you've come from, there *must* have been a bit of something else all the same, a touch of pity . . .'

'Yes, probably. But those who had it won't be there to tell you about it. They're dead. Those who felt pity for others are dead. Those who pitied themselves are dead. And we're all dead. Dead for nothing. We suffered for nothing, absolutely nothing. All pointless. Nothing, nothing that could be of any good. I went there with a decent body, a decent face, fair hair and grey eyes. I come back with a ravaged face, grey hair, a body which I can't bear to look at and which isn't fit to be looked at. All that for nothing, nothing, nothing . . . Yes, there will still be very learned people, but *our* knowledge, our extreme knowledge, our knowledge of the extremes, will be of no use. It's a knowledge without a future because it's not stable, it's not transmissible and can't be handed down, and what use is that? None. Knowledge that's no use to anyone is nothing. And there again, there's no name for it . . .'

Silence. Then she remembered my question.

'Oh yes, laughter. It'll take a course of re-education for the muscles to learn to laugh or smile again properly. It's still possible, though—I do laugh already . . .'

'No, you don't laugh, Klara, you sneer . . .'

'Oh . . . Yes, you're right . . . But I think I could still manage all sorts of laughter—I'm bound to have reasons to laugh. To cry, no. I don't see what could be done to make my tear glands work again, or even if it's necessary. Being unable to cry comes from having lived too long—it's a feature of old age. I remember my grandmother telling me that at her age she had no tears left. They'd all dried up. She didn't seem to mind.'

'And you? Do you mind?'

'Yes. I long for tears again. My tears. Everyone's tears.'

She also told me that at the beginning she and her friends had invented what they called 'the Laughing Wall'. The idea was that during roll-call they should all join in wave after wave of guffaws. Klara thought some of them were killed for that, but after all it couldn't have been worse than going on living as they did. She said all four of them tried to get the others to join in, but they soon gave that up because, among other things, many were afraid, and it was difficult to organise so many people speaking so many different languages. Anyway, some were already very ill, some actually dying, even during the morning and evening roll-calls. It was also a way of organising clean, straightforward deaths. She said they all hoped to die by being shot, but that people always wait until they no longer have any choice. Everyone wants to hold out and hold out, and as a result they all die miserable deaths. But who wants to plan his or her own death, especially in a group? That was madness.

Now she thinks that if the madness of others was destroying them, their own madness might have saved them. Not from death itself, but from a certain kind of death. But she and her friends soon became listless too, more concerned with surviving than with wasting energy on action that might deliberately lead to death. But Klara thought it was a pity not to have tried. She's still convinced there would have been consequences, and many of the prisoners might have died, but at least there'd have been some dignity about it. She insisted that all her friends died in the most abject circumstances except the one from Cracow, who had received slightly better medical care from her doctor friends, but it's only because it was Auschwitz that one can say that, since, objectively speaking, the friend from Kracow also died abjectly, even if she was wearing a clean nightdress.

And the question is, she added, were all these people born somewhere in one of the countless little places all over Europe, just to be shoved into a gas chamber in Upper Silesia, to burn and vanish into thin air like a cigarette, said Klara, or to die in their own excreta, covered with lice, each one alone on a straw pallet matted with filth?

I'm tired.

Yesterday the young man, Legris, phoned Alban. He'd like to meet Klara to ask her to forgive him. He seems to be obsessed with his blunder. Alban promised to mention it to her if he could, but warned him it might not be possible. He asked how she was. Alban told him she was sleeping a bit better.

That's hardly true. She's started walking around the living-room again at night and taking a short nap at odd moments during the day. You can't really say she sleeps normally. On the other hand, she does eat more, though still very little. Fabienne and Alban have worked out a treatment, mostly vitamins and things to stimulate the appetite, because the result of her tests is very unsatis-factory. It's surprising that she bears up so well. Alban says it's a good thing they don't know all the answers, because really she ought to be taking a complete rest. Which she isn't.

Klara talks to me, talks to us about another planet, with its own customs, classes, codes, rituals and sacrifices . . .

another planet. A terrifying one. A planet with nothing familiar in it to give us mental access except our own instincts, though it's impossible to imagine we would ever follow them to such extremes. I find it difficult to believe all she tells me. To believe it's really true. I'm quite disposed to trust Klara, but what she says is like a fiction, a grotesque legend belonging to some remote undiscovered tribe, whereas it really concerns people quite close to us, close enough to touch, who might be ourselves, perpetrators and victims or both at the same time, as seems quite possible. We're learning that anything is possible, even where we ourselves are concerned. That's probably the most frightening thing about it all, and the most painful to listen to. Alban and I have discussed it over and over, and have arrived at that conclusion. We find it hard to make sense of Klara's stories, though really the drift is quite clear. Yet something in us refuses to accept it. In me especially.

How, for instance, is one to understand what she says about fear? Sometimes fear is a factor, at least as far as I can see. Yet she often says she wasn't afraid: for example, she says, 'When anything may happen, you're afraid; but when everything has happened, you're not afraid any more.' Many people were afraid, but not she, or very little; sometimes her hair would stand on end, but not from apprehension. Even when it was a matter of blows: the first time is terrible, she said, but all the other times you force yourself to think of something else. It's only the body that hurts; the mind is elsewhere.

She and her friends agreed to give names to the forty-five kinds of clouds in the five different languages they spoke. They spent some time agreeing on the names, repeating them, and then making up words out of the first or second letters of each name, and so on, then doing the same with the names spelled backwards. The girl from Linz was quickest at this game.

Right up to the end, Klara told me, the clouds helped them get through the blows, the screams, the lack of privacy—the last time, at the beginning of January this year, through the hanging of the four girls.

'In the end, when I was alone, I took care to repeat the names to myself regularly, and I went on doing it when I was in Cracow, Prague, Linz and Berlin. The last days in the camp were days of hope and therefore of doubt, new sufferings that did nothing to lessen the others. Yes, the last days were frightful, and about them I can speak freely without having to correct myself, because we were going to return to the normal world, and I was afraid again.'

She gave me the list of clouds. One is missing.

She spoke about the first time she herself was beaten.

'It was a Polish bitch with her whip. She lashed out at me. I suppose I must have done something wrong, I don't know what, I don't remember, but my friend from Prague, who was behind me, caught hold of me by the neck and twisted me round, and hit me again twice. That was what saved me. She told me I was just about to jump at the bitch, she could tell from my back; she was sure; and if I had, the Polish woman would have knocked me down and beaten me to death. The funny thing was that after this incident my friend from Prague was made a *blockova*. The stupid bitch with the whip thought my friend was trying to be cooperative in order to get a job.

'I was so shocked I didn't even try to protect myself. It was too much, not the blows, I don't remember them, but that she should do that, that it should be her who took over and beat me, that was the most unthinkable part of it . . .'

It was on January 6 this year that the four girls were hanged. Klara saw it. They all had to watch.

I'm copying out the list of clouds, as Klara dictated them. She listed them all in French.

'Watchtower Smoke Syringe Hoof Pick-axe Tribunal Knickers Whip Soap House Dog Photo Revolver Dysentery Fire Scissors Shin Train Bowl Typhus Turnip Latrines Sun Coat Soup Lawyer Bed Child Straightline Coal Blanket Phenol Wool Fly Bathroom Rat Moustache Tooth Stove Lice Screams Skull America Barbed-wire.'

Léandre arrived the day before yesterday. He's staying with us. Louise is still at La Roseraie. So I've found out what Alban knew more or less already. In October '43 Louise and Léandre took in two brothers aged fourteen and eleven and their cousin, a girl of nine, all three from Le Mans. The two fathers came back in January, but the mothers and the boys' little sister all died at Auschwitz. Léandre told me rather a confused story. He seemed a bit embarrassed, and in the end I asked him why.

'It's because I'm ashamed, because I'm still ashamed . . . when I took the children home in January I couldn't look the two fathers in the face. Physically . . . how is it possible . . . the men without their wives . . . and the children without their mother . . . Imagine it, Angélika—imagine how unbearable it was . . . I was ashamed to be a Frenchman . . .'

I couldn't understand why he'd got himself into that state. Léandre gives the impression of being a jovial and outgoing person, not at all pessimistic. I pointed out that the risks he and Louise had taken for the children did them honour, and I couldn't see why he should be ashamed. It took him some time to answer.

'You see, Angélika, perhaps you don't know, and my son certainly won't have told you, but . . . I used to be anti-Semitic. That's the truth—you might as well know it . . . and . . . I wasn't very keen on my son mixing with you and your brother and his wife. I didn't say anything . . . or not much . . . but Alban knows . . . True, I got you your papers . . . and I'd have done the same for your brother and his wife . . . but mainly to protect Alban . . . I like to be helpful too . . . and for people to be grateful to me . . . all that . . . But, Angélika, the shame . . . and you should know that Louise helped change me, too. She made me find out about the anti-Jewish laws . . . and then I was filled with shame . . . shame, shame such as I could never have imagined . . . and anger too, against Pétain, against Laval . . . above all against myself . . . fundamentally against myself . . .'

Poor Léandre, he was hiding his face in his hands. He went on explaining.

'I was just an ordinary, stupid anti-Semite . . . In business we're all ruthless, but if you're in competition with a Jew you say—*I* used to say, "dirty Jew." I used to think "dirty Jew" even if I didn't say it; I really thought it . . . and all that follows . . . People don't do each other any favours, that's just part of the profession whether you're open and above-board or not. I was just like all the others, so why did I think "dirty Jew"? Angélika, all those thoughts led to the laws that I read, that were applied, and that led to deportations, the deaths of children and women and old men—all the dirty little thoughts of dirty disgusting Frenchmen . . . The fact is, I thought I was decent, and I find I was an accomplice in all those crimes . . . Right, I'll stop now, and I shan't talk about it again. But you'll know about it, Angélika. But know too that you're welcome in our family, and the little girl too, and . . . please forgive me . . .'

It was rather embarrassing, and struck me as exaggerated, but he speaks as his character dictates. I just said not to worry, and that I thanked him for confiding in me, and that I had nothing to forgive him for because he hadn't done anything against me personally.

It's true I hadn't known them very well, but all our meetings had been cordial. When I wanted to change my identity, Alban had asked his father and Léandre had managed it quickly and I thought willingly. I never sensed any dislike or reluctance. On the contrary, I remember Louise as very warm and friendly—and Léandre the same.

People are very complicated.

Alban has told us about Jérôme Legris, but Klara doesn't want to meet him. She said: 'I've no wish to see that foolish young man again—I don't forgive imbeciles. In any case, it wasn't me he insulted, so how can I forgive words that have nothing to do with me? What he needs to do is find the shaven woman he did insult. Tell him from me to go and apologise to one of the women who did have their heads shaved, instead of trying to salve his conscience on me. Don't let's talk about it any more!'

I must say I agree. I too think the young man is trying to let himself off lightly. His attitude is facile, and as unseemly as his attack itself.

I didn't see anything of the outrages that were committed in the rue de Rennes. If those women really were traitors, they could have been tried in court. If they'd slept with 'the enemy', after all that's no more despicable than going to work for him in Germany.

Strange. The day before yesterday I was telling Léandre that I had nothing to forgive him for because I hadn't been hurt personally. Klara's reaction towards Legris is the same. As if neither of us was affected by the offence—as if it were just a matter of hitting the wrong target. We don't see ourselves as targets. Is it because we don't want to suffer? Are we really so unaware? We never mention the Jews. Even Klara doesn't, despite all she's been through. I don't either, don't even think about them. Not really, or only vaguely. And my attitude isn't forced. It's as if we hadn't internalised the connection. Fairly late in the day, we found out we were Jews, but I never understood why, when we weren't registered. I didn't find out till I was twelve. Mother found it rather awkward to explain what it meant to be Jewish. Her own parents were non-practising. Perhaps her grandparents remained faithful to the old religion, but she never knew them. In short, it was a confusing situation for all of us, and nothing was ever done to clear it up. The few explanations that Mother gave us always ended, 'Anyhow, it's madness pure and simple.'

For Klara it was more painful and more fundamental. Her father—I think he was an army officer at the time— asked for a divorce in '33. Klara came to our house in tears. I didn't understand what was going on. Mama said, 'Your mother's a Jewess, Klara dear, that's all.' Klara shook her head, and I just looked at her. I was trying as hard as I could to see the connection between Jewishness and divorce. It took me some time to accept that parents could separate because of that. How atrocious! And Klara adored her father. Ullrich Adler loved his wife and daughter too. At least, that was what we'd always had reason to think. Herr

Adler and Papa were close, not exactly friends, but both veterans of the 1914 war. Papa was an army doctor, and his medals made it possible for us to go on with our studies until we left Germany. All the same, this divorce was outrageous. People said there were lots like them. Mother told us so too, and consoled herself every time with the thought that our own father was dead: 'At least he won't have to go through that.'

Some time later we heard what was probably the true version. Herr Adler hadn't asked outright for a divorce, simply suggested he'd have to leave the army and so his career would be finished. Frau Adler is supposed to have said jokingly, 'All right then, ask for a divorce!' and he, timidly, to have shown his real wishes by answering something like, 'Would you agree?' Frau Adler, hurt, proud and angry, did all she could to speed up the procedure, making her own conditions. Her husband accepted them all, probably only too glad to do something to make himself feel less guilty. She took back all her property, including the apartment in Berlin that she'd inherited from her parents. Klara never saw her father again. Presumably that too was part of the arrangement. Three years later, Klara and Rainer got married. Klara's insistence overcame all the arguments of Rainer and the two mothers. I know she let her father know too. Was that a challenge? By marrying a complete Jew—because apparently *we* are out-and-out Jews!—she was making it quite impossible for him to protect her, always supposing he wanted to. Ullrich Adler married again in '35, and before we left Germany he already had two children, a boy and a girl. Frau Adler—Margarethe Schwartz —knew about it. Strangely enough, her ex-husband has always kept her informed about his new life.

Apart from the day when she cried, Klara never spoke to me about this episode. She may have told Rainer more, but now I rather doubt it.

Klara's obstinacy. Her loyalty to her mother and to her mother's name. The cowardice of her father. The contrast. And so on.

One could write a chapter on loyalty: Klara and I interpreted it in different ways. I soon decided to change my identity: my new name was Solange Blanc.

We'd been brought up to adore George Sand. She was our grandmother's favourite author, and my mother was called Aurore after the writer herself, while her brother's first name was Maurice, after the Maréchal de Saxe, Sand's ancestor . . . We'd read *François le Champi* and *La Mare au Diable* when we were very young, and later on *Consuelo* and of course *Lélia*. Naturally, I chose Solange, like George Sand's daughter, another way of remaining my own mother's daughter. Le Blanc was the name of a place in le Berry, the region where Sand had a country house—Lisa had told us about it in Berlin, but the kind forgers left out the 'le' on my passport. I'd taken a lot of time and trouble making up this name, which rather amused Rainer. However, I know he'd have liked to change his identity too, but Klara was against it. All the same, when he was working under cover, he called himself René Leroux. What a farrago! Solange is rather a sweet name, like Ilse. You could translate it as the angel of the sun, or the sun of the angel. Lisa told me she was the patron saint of le Berry. I like that.

Klara's loyalty proved lethal. Our names were lethal, our ancestors transformed into deadly poison. Solange Blanc saved my life. We've taken steps to make it official. Then we'll get married!

Rainer, Rainer, Rainer—this need to keep writing your name.

Klara's jewels are almost sold. Léandre is supposed to finish off the whole transaction in a couple of days. Apparently he's made a good bargain. I feel tired. I miss Victoire. It's hot. Nothing goes right. One must just stick it out.

I miss Agathe too. She's very busy, and I don't like to disturb her. We talk on the phone. I'd like to spend a long evening with Agathe . . . Later on, perhaps.

Klara has cut her hair again, but not too much. Now it seems to me it rather suits her like that. Her cheeks are not so hollow as they were. Perhaps she'll get her pretty oval-shaped face back. Apparently she's put on a kilo in weight, which is a sign of improving health. She still sleeps on the couch and walks about at night. She nibbles away at her food a bit more, but as if reluctantly. She remains faithful to the glass of hot milk with sugar in it, though. During the day, she wanders around Paris. She sets out quite early, at about eight, and comes back, she tells me, at about five in the afternoon. The other day, for the first time, she asked me if she should buy something for dinner. I was surprised. Pleasantly surprised. I admit it hadn't even occurred to me. As regards practical things, Klara needs older people around her, like Louise and Adeline (and as in the case of Fabienne and the glass of milk). I'm not what people here consider a capable woman. Our relationship used to be one of friendship. Now, apart from a few brief moments, I can't see my old friend as she was, so I feel at a loss. All I can do is listen, if she feels like talking. She doesn't always want to. I don't press her.

I confine myself to that role. Before the war—that is, in the old days—we always used to talk a lot, but then it was Klara who listened.

I asked her what she did all day in Paris. She said she took photographs. I probably looked surprised; I've never seen her take her cameras with her.

'I don't use a camera. They're still too heavy for me. Eyes are enough, as they were in Brzezinka. There, I and my friend from Prague took photos like that. We made ourselves take at least one every day—a good one, some-times two. And every day we told one another about them; we called that developing them. We could do that when we had decent jobs.'

'What do you mean, decent jobs?'

'When I was ill with dysentery in December '42 . . . but I

won't tell you any more about that disgusting filth . . . I said I spoke four languages and had studied medicine for three years. My medical studies didn't count for much—there were no medicines or equipment to treat people with anyway . . . It was then that I met my friend from Cracow. There were no jobs available then, but she managed to get me into "Canada". (She explained that this was what they called the store where the clothes of the deportees and the contents of their suitcases were kept. Alban suggested that this strange name was a sort of equivalent for "El Dorado".) Later on my job there was given to my friend from Prague, and I was sent to the infirmary. Finally, my friend from Linz replaced me there, and I went to Reception because of my Russian and German.

'In all these jobs one could organise things a bit; that is, there were things you could exchange in order to be better clothed—mainly shoes and woollen goods. Shoes—you can't imagine how important they were. Your feet could be the death of you. Good shoes could save you . . . So, we took photos, my friend from Prague and I, and developed them. But although we had similar subjects, our pictures were rarely alike. She often took close-ups, while I tended towards general views with objects strewn about to the right of the frame. My friend from Prague puzzled her brains to find out what these objects meant, and why they were on the right. I told her her close-ups meant she didn't want to see reality. We didn't have much time for these activities, so our comments weren't very profound. I've thought about them since . . . I've tried . . . since I've been back in Paris . . . I've been looking for a subject for a photo. Before she died, my friend from Prague said, "Take a photo of peace for me." So I'm searching.'

'And you can't find what you want? . . .'

'No . . . yesterday I was in the sixteenth *arrondissement* . . . in a very steep street with a view of the Seine. A quiet street with a house standing back from the road, with sculptures on the façade and a bow-window. There was a little garden in front, with railings round it. The rusty iron gate, which was shut, was painted pale green; the paint was flaking off. With the sun shining down on it all, it looked very pretty, very peaceful. I'm not going to develop it, though I did just snap it on the off-chance . . . But on the way home it occurred to me that you could hang yourself on those railings, like some French poet whose name I forget . . . hang yourself, or be badly hurt . . . And finally, I thought, a gate that's shut isn't very pleasant when you're outside . . . or inside, for that matter. In short, I destroyed that photograph.'

'Can you develop another one for me?'

She looked at me, hesitated for a long while, then came to a decision.

'If you like . . . but it's more an image than a photo . . . I didn't actually take it, I wasn't thinking in terms of photos. It was near Strasbourg, I was on the train . . . a vision . . . a rope stretched out between two trees, with clothes hanging on it, blowing to and fro just in order to be clean, to smell fresh, and to dry. That was what I found most reassuring. That was peace, I thought. Peace again; the opposite of war. For me, at that moment, *that* was peace—a meadow, with washing drying quietly on a line hung between two trees in an orchard on a calm summer afternoon. Afterwards, I too was able to sleep, like washing on a line.'

Then, as often, there was a long silence. She was pondering. I was thinking of her image.

'But there must have been washing drying just as quietly all the time I was over there in the camps . . . Then came that image near Strasbourg . . . but that doesn't make it a photo of peace. With a washing-line you can strangle someone, or hang yourself. With the washing too.'

'Any photos of people? Children?'

'No. Two people . . . from one moment to the next they can fly at each other's throats . . . all the people you pass in the street . . . each one is a possible murderer . . . No, that kind of photo is out of the question . . . after Oswiecim, to show a person is to show a war, a potential crime, or one already committed . . .'

'What about flowers?'

'Some gardener's pride—I don't want them . . . A tree perhaps.'

'But you can hang yourself on that!'

A croak of laughter from Klara.

~

'You're right . . . Mission impossible . . .'

Silence.

'A wild-flower perhaps. And yet . . . nothing that threatens or is threatened can be an image of peace. The sea threatens, a cliff is threatened . . . and threatens too . . . peace in between two threats, if you like, but nothing permanent . . . perhaps some dead bodies . . . but not from back there, not corpses from the camps . . . Peaceful corpses, who died an easy death . . . a dead child . . . perhaps that's it . . . I don't really see any solution . . . I probably shan't be able to keep my promise . . . nothing that's alive can represent peace, unless you just say it does, arbitrarily, and leave it at that. But the whole thing would be a sham . . . It was a stupid request, and a stupid promise . . .'

Later she told me she didn't develop all her photos, and suspected that her friend didn't either, but they never talked about it (*we* 'selected' too, she said with a bitter smile, alluding to the way the Germans chose among the new prisoners to allocate them to instant death). Some scenes were impossible to photograph, she added, then was silent. I felt I couldn't question her further. I thought of some things she'd told me one day which I'd been unable to write down. Women on all fours, licking up some soup that had been spilt on the ground . . . a woman who'd fallen down and was being torn to pieces by a dog, urged on by his SS minder . . . and what Klara had said about the camp where the gipsies were kept, and the gipsy children . . . That evening, Klara had turned pale, almost grey. I think she was about to faint. I asked her not to go on.

Since then she's prowled about all the time, and it's been hard for me to sleep too.

Next day, I asked her to forgive me. She said, 'I understand.'

Later, talking to Alban, she said, 'Of all the atrocities, what happened to the gipsy children was the most horrifying.'

Alban is braver than I am. He regards it as his duty to hear everything. Sometimes I wonder whether, instead of freeing Klara, talking to her about her experiences doesn't force her to stay back there in the camps. Alban doesn't know either, but given that there's a doubt he prefers to listen and even to encourage her to talk. We've both noticed that she never or hardly ever repeats herself. Sometimes she'll go back to certain points, but only to explain them or make them clearer, never really to repeat them.

Whenever I look at her, at her eyes, remember what those eyes have seen . . . I think of what Alban says:

'If people don't believe the victims, the perpetrators can get away with anything.'

Muslims—that was the name in the camp for people at the end of their tether—weak, devoid of feeling, indifferent to everything but food; reduced to a degree of suffering that nullifies all pain and renders it indifferent, if that's conceivable. A terrifying state, according to Klara. All the others dreaded becoming like them. It could happen to anybody from one day to the next. They watched over one another, friends helped friends. Those who had no friends— loners—couldn't survive—their state was unimaginable.

An un-human state, Klara called it.

'I, even as I am, couldn't play the part of a Muslim woman in a film . . . I'm obese in comparison—all the ex-detainees would laugh. No film will ever be able to depict those people. They were the only ones who'd managed to go somewhere else, I don't know where, but somewhere else. We'd all passed many, many limits, far too many, but they, the Muslims, had gone even further, far far away, where no one wants to go . . . imagine being in the most miserable condition possible, a state so wretched, so humiliating, so totally abject . . . that it inspires neither pity nor compassion . . . only disgust or anger . . . it's loneliness unconscious of loneliness, the greatest of all solitudes . . . endless, bottomless cruelty, absolute desolation.'

Malnutrition ate up the bones and hollowed the cheeks of the gipsy children. Klara saw it. That's another thing that makes her wander about every night.

After she'd spoken about the photographs, she said:

'Back there it was a misfortune to have eyes, but we all kept our eyes in order to see . . . and not to see . . . it's the same thing. It's also a misfortune to have ears to hear, and we did hear. Sounds are harder to forget than images; sounds can recur anywhere, at any time—creaks, screams, trains, whistles, death-rattles, music, weeping, murmurs, barking—of dogs and of men—they're the same. But images have to be deliberately conjured up. Here there's nothing to recall all that . . . except nightmares.'

For a long time we didn't say anything. Both our ashtrays were full. She spoke in a rasping voice.

'What to forgive, or whom, or for what, it's impossible to say. As I've told you, nothing really applies to that world. No, forgiveness has no meaning. Can a word give meaning to something that has none itself? . . . Is it even desirable that it should? . . . Those who think so will always be attempting a mere approximation, and be in continual doubt . . . Isn't that true? As far as I'm concerned, the rest of my life won't be long enough for me to be sure I didn't dream it all . . . the nightmare of an idiot, a *détraqué*, a crazy person . . . because we were all *traqués*, hunted down, even those who were privileged . . . but when we came out we were *détraqués*, crazy . . . *détraqués* because we'd been *traqués* . . . As for forgiveness . . . the idea of forgiveness . . . that would be to exonerate *oneself*, to exonerate *myself* . . . and that makes no sense. In such a state of ignominy, the mere thought of forgiveness collapses, it's obscene. There has to be a status quo so that the world can go on living . . . The idea of forgiveness would kill the world . . .

'I'm now in a state of incomprehension about the world—incomprehension and disbelief. And of disbelief about myself. I myself have become a world to which I have no access, which I can't understand . . . It's the same with revenge . . . Imagine, what would you avenge, upon whom, and to what degree of abjection and cynicism would you go? . . . No. Let the people responsible for all that sort it out for themselves. The numbers they tattooed on us will be transferred to them and their descendants, that's how *I* imagine it . . . but it's not certain, and anyway it's nothing to do with me.'

Sometimes, though, Klara pronounces judgments, peremptory like all judgments. I think I remember one of them exactly:

'It's just as hard to make yourself despise the human race as it is to make yourself admire it.' Hmm.

~

Later.

'Is a question a thought? . . . one might think so, yet I'm obsessed by a question not inspired by any thought. What I keep going over and over are images without thought, images and yet more images . . . calling for a question mark that I don't even add . . . at the end there's a void where the question might be, then a flash-back to some images, and so on and on. I don't know anything. I don't know anything any more.'

This evening before we parted we were talking about torturers, and she let out an enigmatic comment: 'Who can say if we were in their dreams or they in ours . . . and it's not over yet . . .'

I was too tired to ask why 'or' and not 'and'.

Perhaps she made a mistake. I must get some sleep. I can't take any more.

Léandre's leaving the day after tomorrow. Alban explained that he had a lot of apartments in Paris, and a whole block of them further away in the avenue Henri-Martin.

'Don't you worry about him—in a few days he'll have got everything organised and found someone to do the house-work.'

I realise now that Alban is more than discreet about his parents, and almost reticent when it comes to talking about his father. I told him about the conversation on Léandre's first day. He made no comment. I was a bit surprised, but didn't press him. When Alban doesn't want to say anything, he has his own way of changing the subject. On this occasion he announced that he was soon going to leave La Salpêtrière to specialise in pediatrics. He's talked it over at length with his boss, who agrees. He's only got to find a replacement first and show him the ropes. Now that he'd made up his mind, he was ready to tell me how much of a shock and a revelation Victoire's birth had been to him— that was the determining factor, but he was also influenced, right through the war and up to the present, by all the children he's treated, whom he feels unable to help properly. He's afraid of making mistakes. He spoke to me about how children suffer, physically and above all psychologically, and the quasi-impossibility of relieving their suffering, through shortage of time and lack of competence. He reminded me that Rainer had talked to him a lot about the work of Freud and Melanie Klein, and about his own wish to specialise in that field after the war. He also told me how he missed Rainer's friendship more and more.

We talked again about the birth of Victoire.

Alban was anxious. It was his first *accouchement* without professional assistance. The only help he had was me, and it was my first time too. To be exact, it would be the first time for all four of us! We'd had everything ready in the apartment for a week. Klara was calm and gentle—*she* reassured *us*. We probably showed how nervous we were in spite of ourselves. But all went well. Klara bit hard on a table napkin to keep herself from crying out—we wanted to attract as little attention as possible. Agathe, who was just getting over the birth of Isidore, stood by ready to phone one of Alban's colleagues in case of difficulty.

I remember how thrilled we both were when Victoire's head appeared. Afterwards, Klara was thrilled too, and radiant. I can see her now—her long fair hair soaking wet, her dazzling smile. Now I might describe it as a 'look of victory'. A faint false note sounded deep in my head at Klara's rather cool 'All that's missing is the father.' Amid all

Klara's enthusiastic cries of 'Lika, Lika, Alban, you've been marvellous, thank you, thank you', there was that phrase: not 'Rainer', but 'the father'. Already, probably, a secret resentment.

I sometimes tend to gloss over what bothers me. When it's too much for me I dodge it altogether and don't try to write it down, but the little I do write does me a power of good.

Writing definitely brings me relief, but also more and more pleasure. I try not to misrepresent Klara's words, and above all her thoughts.

Yes, at that time she still used to say Lika, Alban, Rainer, Agathe . . . it took me several days to notice when she stopped using names or any other polite forms. We went on addressing her as Klara.

At the beginning, I wrote that the first words she said were, 'Hallo, Angélika, how are you?' Now I'm no longer sure. Perhaps she only said, 'Hallo, how are you?' Did she even say hallo? Why would she have said it that day, and never again since?

She doesn't call out to me in the ordinary way from one room to another. She either shouts or comes to me herself. She enters my bedroom without knocking. One night I was undressing, but she didn't apologise, she just said, 'I don't like undressing now.' Jokingly, I said, 'What about when you have a bath?' She said, 'The water covers you up, but it's disagreeable to have to get out.'

So no trace of politeness now, no thank you, please,

sorry, good morning, goodnight, still less any *bon appétit*! Or any other considerate ways of acting or asking. We were all brought up to be polite; with us this meant being natural and adaptable to circumstances; Klara was taught to be more formal and rather stilted.

Now courtesy has completely disappeared as far as she's concerned, and she keeps to that attitude so strictly that it seems like a challenge, or at least the result of a deliberate and unwavering decision.

I asked her what it was that Agathe had said.

Apparently, when Klara was going down the stairs with the two gendarmes, Agathe leaned over the banisters and called out: 'I'll look after the turtle-dove.'

That was what Agathe had said: 'I'll look after the turtle-dove.'

We were both silent for a long time.

But when we parted for the night, Klara said:

'Tell her she saved the French language . . . after that, I neither heard nor remembered anything of what happened when I was in Drancy. I clung on to what she'd said, tell her . . . right up until I left *la douce France*.'*

---

*[*Tr.* 'sweet' or 'gentle' France, a common and affectionate way of referring to the country as one's historical homeland; here presumably ironical.]

For some time I've wondered whether Klara still reads and writes. There are plenty of books in the rue Richer, but I've never seen a book lying about in the sitting-room. Yesterday evening I asked her about it. She told me she couldn't read any more. 'Or else it would have to be books that are comic, innocent and comic. That's about all I could read, and even that I can't manage yet.'

She thought for a bit.

'It would have to be something like . . . once upon a time there were three charming girls, thin and with shaven heads. A fat bitch with hair happened to pass by. One of these charming ones stuck out her foot and splosh! the fine fat creature fell in the shit. The three young ladies got hold of some sticks and, laughing, beat her on the head, her fine head of a bitch. Whenever she struggled free they hit her again, laughing and laughing as they beat her down. That's what's regarded as funny in Oswiecim, you see. Everything we laughed at there isn't called funny anywhere else, except perhaps in slapstick comedy . . . but it really makes no difference to me if that was a farce or not.'

Silence.

'So what is it about that episode that does interest you?'
    'Knowing that that was the last time I laughed. That that was the moment, the place and the occasion of my last laugh . . . That's what Brzezinka was like . . .'
    'Brzezinka—that's Birkenau, isn't it?'
    (I knew it was, but I wanted to provoke a reaction.)
    'Yes, but I won't utter another word of German.'
    'That's impossible, Klara!'
    'No more impossible than living there, or coming back from there; but the improbable is possible. Inside the impossible there's always a little possible.'

What followed is like a settling of accounts with the German language, the Germans in general, and the Jews as well.

Klara never speaks a word of German (apart from the odd slip of the tongue, which she hastily tries to cover up), not even for expressions peculiar to the camps which I'd heard already at the Lutétia when the prisoners first started coming back. They used to intersperse their stories with German words, but Klara never did. Sometimes her speech would slow down, which at first I took for a new habit, arising from the need to cover lapses of memory or to avoid painful memories or formulate them carefully. But now I realise it's due to her sustained effort to get round the language problem, and her determination never to let it be obvious.

'Quick, quick, quick,' she tells me. 'Think the word in German, but don't say it whatever you do.'

I think, 'Schnell, schnell, schnell.'

'The rest of my life won't be long enough for me to kill that language in me. Day after day I'll cut down the tiny shoots that grow again, that'll be bound to grow again until there's no sap left. Then perhaps I'll die . . . If I were to speak German again I'd be afraid it would suddenly bark back in my face. All the Germans will have to live with that threat. But the German people will always be my people, and the German nation my nation; even if I never write or speak another word of German, that language is always weeping inside me.' (That's what she said: weeping.) 'They made it bark—the language of Goethe, of Schiller, Hölderlin, Heine, Fontane, Kant and of a whole people. They barked so loud that the echo of it never dies away. And yet it was in that language that I last hummed a tune . . . Reluctantly, I'll hold on to the tune and try to forget the words. But there's a part of me that won't be able to turn traitor. I'm stuck with the accent. It can't be cast off; I'm branded with it for life, for death. The German language irrigates my brain, it's mine, mine, do you see—the language of my childhood, of my father and mother; and of generations of my relations, of all my grandparents and ancestors, who made promises and swore oaths to one another in it, who stammered, lied, sang us to sleep in it, and died in their German beds uttering German words, surrounded by loved ones who consoled them and mourned in German. In German and only in German.'

Afterwards, Klara talked about the camp, where it was preferable, if not absolutely necessary, to know German.

'I used my language as if it was my body, a humiliated body; treated German like a despised body, prostituted my language, yes, used my mother tongue like a whore, exploited the very colour of my language, the accent, which I've never lost in any other language except Russian. My language, my beloved language, was used for that, to save my skin . . . I pushed it in front of me, making it wiggle its behind, yes, as vulgar as that—don't look at me with that expression—every time I'd tell her, come on, slut, give the SS the glad eye, come on, diddle the SS, stuff like that . . . telling myself, if she helps to kill, she can also help me to live, she can be useful in all sorts of ways, this trollop . . . but sometimes she was like a child, and I would rock her in my arms, reciting nursery rhymes, poems, conscientiously cleansing her of all dirt or taint, wiping her bottom, telling her, you're the real thing too, you'll be that again, but now it's too awful, so I spit on you too.'

Klara reels this off in a monotone, her words are like a

river bearing along rocks, gravel, dead bodies and ruins alike, pell-mell—detritus to be swept away indiscriminately. For me all this is simply fantastic and unreal: Klara herself washed ashore to catalogue it all. Here for that purpose, apparently. If not, why?

'For us Germans it was sometimes necessary to tell ourselves it wasn't our language, to try to imagine that was so. All the others will forget when they go home, or at least they won't still remember those words of violence, words belonging to a particular space and time, not to their rediscovered daily life, words, not a language, words that were just an interlude in the vocabulary of their lives. But the Germans, victims and victimisers alike, will always have to use that language, to quieten the words that once barked, to agree to say and hear "quick" without fearing for their own skin or threatening the life of someone else . . . That's why I need another language, another country, other landscapes and places, and a long time unlike anything I've known before, which has nothing in it to remind one of Europe. In Oswiecim there was the whole Babel of Europe, except English. Apart from that, yes, all the others.'

Silence.

'So I think I'll learn a dead language, and then perhaps in that I'll be all right. Dead languages don't bark any more. In all the languages that are still spoken it's possible to bark, bark at any moment. People don't do that any more in dead languages. They must have done it once in Latin, ancient Greek, Egyptian, and Sumerian . . . but not now. When a language comes alive again, if we can imagine that for the sake of argument, it can bark. If you give it oxygen, a language can bark. Perhaps it's only natural. I've met some Zionists. They're re-learning Hebrew. The Jews will bark in Hebrew, you'll see, they'll bark in a language that's been safe from it for two thousand years. The language of learning, chanting and prayer will start barking again like any other language. Perhaps it's only natural. Perhaps everything about all this business is only natural . . .'

I haven't mentioned before that Klara usually paces about when she's talking, coming back at regular intervals to the table to flick the ash off her cigarette or stub it out. It's by these movements that I can tell how nervous she is—and sometimes how angry. Her voice is usually toneless, but recently, for a week at most, a few variations have appeared. I can detect some slight questionings and even some timid exclamations. But all rather faint still.

What followed was more or less like this:

'The Jews will kill too. We'll have to get used to it. They'll learn how to bark and kill too. If the Jews are a people and have a land, a country, this war will have created one more murderous nation. There's no reason why they shouldn't be as stupid as all the other nations, that's all the good-or-evil I wish them . . .'

'But Klara, you're a Jew too, aren't you? Just as I am, apparently.'

'No more than before. For me it's just as impossible to be Jewish as it is not to be German. They won't have succeeded in making me into a Jew, no . . . to admit that I'm a Jew would be to admit that all those madmen, idiots and perverts are right. They could say, see how right we were, they really are Jews, even if it takes shock treatment to make them remember it. But no—that won't work with me. After a big fire, does everyone have to be either a fireman or an arsonist? Why should I have to answer for my ancestors unto the hundredth generation? And how is the Jewish religion different from all the others? Those old ways are interesting, like any other mythology, but neither more nor less. If you want to know what I really think, it's that Hitler is helping the Jews to remain Jews, or to become Jews again, and that to return to the bosom of Judaism is to pay allegiance to that wretched corporal. I refuse, yes, I refuse with all my might to see anything transcendental about the massacre that's just taken place. It was sheer butchery, nothing more. The reality was more sordid than anything anyone could tell or dream up. Some people will connect it with the history of the downtrodden Hebrew people, the heroes of exile . . . but what will the Gipsies say? People of the Book . . . People without a Book . . . All the chosen peoples get it in the neck sooner or later . . . Pazuzu must have known that. Only that lunatic and some of the Jews themselves still believe in the fable of chosen people. It costs all the others dear. And the idea of a pure race is a pure obscenity, yes, the idea of a swine, of someone without any balls, a maniac, a milksop, or all four in one. You remember that French doctor who wrote completely mad things about the Jews, the Jew-Negroes? I remember . . .'

'Yes, Céline, Ferdinand Céline, we laughed because the language seemed so strange and funny to us, we didn't understand it all. Rainer said he had diarrhoea, but he'd got the orifice wrong, and Alban wanted him to be struck off the list of legitimate medical practitioners.

'As for the doctors . . . as we've learned since . . . We were right to laugh then . . . about anything . . . Yes, we ought to have laughed about all those things, including the Austrian corporal himself. To have taken that idiot seriously is the European countries' worst crime.'

'The crime was first of all Germany's, wasn't it?'

'Yes, of course, but remember how crippled we were by the awful Treaty of Versailles!'

Klara, the incurable German.

Sunday 26/8/45 Rue Richer

It's a month since the hotel Lutétia.

I can remember bits and pieces about Thursday and yesterday, and I'm writing it down as it comes, as they sell ground coffee.

Klara reminded me of Wasserman's novel *The Maurizius Case*, which we used to argue about so much with Rainer. Maurizius, sentenced to twenty years imprisonment for a crime he didn't commit, is pardoned after eighteen years. The young son of the prosecutor who pronounced the sentence makes inquiries in Berlin and finds out that his father has obtained Maurizius' pardon, and the youth rebels against this new injustice. He immediately sees the humiliation involved in the pardon, which confirms the guilt of an innocent man and the cowardice of the law, which instead of admitting its mistake prefers pardon to rehabilitation, regardless of the consequences for the man himself, who cannot go on living. Indeed, a few days after he is set free, Maurizius kills himself.

On Thursday Klara talked about the novel to explain that

there'd be no rehabilitation for the civilian victims who'd escaped; in any case, she said, their so-called liberation was really no such thing.

'We were in the path of the armies, that's all. They didn't do anything special for us. It was just chance that they happened to be passing that way. The top brass didn't alter their strategy, and it's quite conceivable that they regarded us as more of a nuisance than anything else. Anyhow, they hadn't got anything planned. At Oswiecim we could do as we liked. The Russians had absolutely no idea how to deal with the situation—they were afraid of typhus—we had to manage as best we could. That suited me, because I could still walk. So in the confusion I was able to get out, and it helped that I could speak Russian.'

Then she told me she'd got hold of a pass for Cracow, and had spent some time in hospital. There she met a doctor who asked her if she'd speak Russian with his children for a few hours a day. So that's what she did, staying with the doctor's family for the whole of February and the first week of March. She was given a little money and some vitamins, and was able to eat and drink tea and get a reasonable amount of rest, and above all they supplied her with warm clothes, including a pair of trousers belonging to the young son of the family. Relations were cordial if not exactly warm, but that suited her. The doctor's wife, who spoke German, also learned Russian with the children. Everything was for the best, though only temporarily, Klara said. But one day the doctor's wife asked her why she'd been in the camp, and Klara said, 'No reason.' 'That's impossible,' said the woman, 'people are always there for some reason.' 'No reason,' Klara repeated, and the other said obstinately, 'Impossible, I can't believe it.' 'Oh well,' said Klara, 'it was because they found out I was a Jew . . .' Then the other replied, 'So, Klara, it *was* for some reason, you see—no one is there if they're innocent.'

Then Klara threw her tea in the woman's face, followed by the tea-pot, the cups, and everything else on the table. She tried to overturn the table too, and when she couldn't, smashed some other things in the room, then rushed out into the corridor and snatched up the woman's coat. So that's the story of the coat that I took at first for a dog.

Later on she told me why she'd been so furious.

'Back in the camps there were any number of rules and regulations, but such laws as existed were purely arbitrary, and so by definition not laws at all.

'As for what we were made to suffer, we were necessarily innocent. Civil rights were no more, legally abolished. There were no limits to the punishments that could be inflicted on the innocent. That fool of a Polish woman ought to have known it—she was a lawyer.'

Klara says nothing about legal States that enact laws which are legal even though they're abject, and don't even leave open the chance of escape offered by arbitrariness.

~

She hid for a fortnight in Cracow, trying to find a train to get out of Poland. She finally managed to get a ticket to Prague . . . Her whole journey was made up of a series of chances.

'I know how to hide, steal, lie, and even tell the truth—which is the same thing in some circumstances; I've acquired the reflexes to be able to do practically anything I want. I can do all those things I just told you, and such knowledge is very valuable.'

I must have looked a bit dubious, for after a while she said, 'Here I tell only the truth. Now I too have to find out what happened to me.'

And naturally I believe her. I need to believe her.

Yesterday Agathe and I, who've been missing the children, made a quick trip to Barbery. We were both mortified and amused to see that they weren't missing us all that much. Adeline demonstrated her usual tact by putting her head into the car just before Agathe drove off, and saying, 'But we talk about you every day, my dears.' Then we laughed, and made fun of one another all the way home.

I enjoyed those few hours at Barbery, and the drive there and back with Agathe. A real breath of fresh air. Agathe told me I hadn't been looking well, and she isn't all that cheerful either. It's been a trying summer. True, it's peace-time again, but the last five years still hang over us. Not only that, but our consciences trouble us because although our nerves were tried by the war, we didn't suffer much physically. We and Alban have promised ourselves a little holiday after Klara goes. Alban looks worn-out too.

I told Agathe what she's supposed to have called out to Klara down the stairs. She remembered it straight away. She's happy to know those few simple words were a help to

Klara. She's not cross with her any more. She still doesn't understand about Victoire. But who does?

I've come back to my post here in the rue Richer. Reluctantly. Tomorrow I'll write down the conversation we had just now. She told me about Berlin. I don't feel up to it now.

Fabienne's at the rue Richer, so I can write in peace. Alban's on duty.

Yesterday we went to bed at three in the morning. Klara's going on with her story, though with frequent interruptions. She's conjuring up a picture of Berlin, taking me back there, though I myself shall never actually see Berlin in ruins.

She speaks more rapidly now, and uses words more confidently. Her utterances are longer, punctuated by silences almost as long, after which she starts off again as if in a hurry to finish. Sometimes a few words of German sneak in, and then she says, 'Forget that,' and bites her lower lip.

Berlin, then.

'As I had neither laughter nor tears any more, I liked Berlin in ruins, shattered, in shreds . . . yes, I liked Berlin reduced to a heap of rubble . . . I liked the ruins of Berlin. It's nothing but ruins now, and Berlin in ruins belonged to me as much as I belonged to Berlin pre-war. My girlfriends and I could have rebuilt Berlin with hoots of laughter, and would have danced, danced, danced on the bunker in the Hitlerstrasse, all the streets in ruined Berlin are called Pazuzustrasse, and will go on being called Pazuzustrasse.'

A long silence.

'It's much better with Hitler's buildings in ruins. The façades look as if their mascara has run, everything has gone up in flames and been left filthy. What's left looks like monuments to bad temper, but it's as if the space inside was glad to be out in the air again. The ground breathes more freely now, the outraged soil of Germany. In fact, all these ruins are a good thing for the Germans—now they can build afresh. They'll have enough to do coping with what will never change . . . their language, their climate, their memories . . . (Silence.)

'Now the Germans ought to tear each other's guts out, but I know them, they won't. They won't even despair.'

I said, 'You exaggerate.'

She said, 'No, of course not—you don't know anything about it.'

I didn't answer.

Then she told me about the Berliners who rummage through the ruins.

'Women and children mostly, they look like some kind of animal, like stray dogs, or free birds (she said *'für Vogel frei'*, probably meaning vagabonds), or like those horrible creatures that live in the desert, or like crows, vultures or other scavengers. When the women bend down you can see their fat thighs—always fat ones, or at least I never saw any thin ones. (With Klara, you know what that means!) Not many men. They haven't got any weapons now . . . And *they're* not going to heave stones about; they're waiting for the bulldozers.

'You know, those women will take anything—bits of broken chairs, scraps of cloth, crockery (broken, of course), disgusting things; they don't want to go on having nothing, so they collect any old refuse, waste or rubbish; they don't realise what they're doing—they just must have things around them in their cellars, as well as their children, if there are any left. They're mothers and old women, I didn't see many old men. Those who look like old women may not be as old as all that, given the age of their children. The children scavenge as well, but more as if they were treasure-hunting, and they're never older than about fifteen. What the women do is more like random, hit-or-miss looting or pilfering, they're not the type to organise their harvest into some kind of trade, they've nothing commercial in mind. To sell things you have to think ahead and calculate, and they don't think, still less calculate. They just hunt and gather, like their prehistoric ancestors, so it was primitives I, a primitive myself, was observing, and like a primitive I threatened them, to drive them away. They would have done the same thing, to kill me. They'd have thrown stones at me—there were plenty of those—but I had a lead pipe in my hand, and I called them scum in the vilest Pankow accent, and they were frightened . . .

'I didn't take anything, I just wanted to harass them, harass some Germans. That's what they've become: a nation of vagrants, a den of thieves, with the same cruelty and innocence, the same ruthlessness and indifference. Rats, a nation of rats, but cowardly rats . . .'

Later she told me of another such encounter on a hill of rubble (her expression). It must have been a very violent scene, because her account of it was very complicated and jerky, stopping and starting, halting, then going on again— too complex and convoluted for me really to remember all the details. I'm trying to put some order into the story, not that it's incoherent—jumbled is more the word for it.

A woman—a bitch, Klara called her—who was sifting through the debris, straightening up and crouching down again without taking her eyes off Klara, groped with her hand and getting hold of a stone, a shapeless lump taken up at random, suddenly stood up, both determined and doubtful—determined about what she wanted to do, doubtful about what she held crumbling in her hand. Three children were gathered round her, trying to keep their balance on the detritus; and it all happened in a second, Klara said—in a second they all four coalesced into a solid mass, indistinguishable from one another in the failing light.

But the mass split up and then re-formed: one child was behind the tallest figure, one was in front, and another to the side, so that all that remained to be seen was one tall shape and one shorter one, and the woman's hand clenched into a fist, which Klara guessed at rather than saw. All four figures swiftly froze. The scene might have lasted a few moments, long enough for Klara to insult the woman and tell her to clear off double quick, meanwhile taking out her revolver to show she meant business. Because of her recently-acquired knowledge, she knew the sort of threat that's most effective, so she shouted something like, 'It's not you, it's one of your . . . that I'm going to . . .' The woman pushed her children aside, stood in front of them, withdrew crab-like behind the mound, and disappeared.

'I didn't take any of the horrible rubbish she'd collected. I just wanted to watch the sun set . . . a malevolent twilight . . . just for me . . .

> *Deutschland, bleiche Mutter!*
> *Wie haben deine Söhne dich zugerichtet*
> *Dass du unter den Völkern sitzest*
> *Ein Gespött oder eine Furcht'*

> [Germany, pale mother!
> What have your sons done to you
> That you have become the laughing-stock
> Or the terror of all nations!]

~

After this story (or whatever it was), and given the nervous state Klara was in, I didn't feel like making any comment. What would have been the point? But I did ask her if she really had a gun. Yes, she's had a revolver ever since Auschwitz, but she hasn't any ammunition left. A brief silence—probably tinged with scepticism—made her pull her little red case out from far back under the divan. She showed me the article in question . . .

'I know you don't quite believe me,' she said, 'but here I don't tell lies.'

I remembered that Klara's father had taught her how to shoot. I seem to recall that Klara enjoyed these lessons. She confirmed this a bit later in the evening, when, no doubt because of the revolver, we both at once thought of Ullrich Adler. She was closing the case, and without looking up, her hands still on the lock, she said, 'I saw my father there . . . at Oswiecim . . .'

My head was in a whirl. After the revolver I was ready to believe anything. As she just stood there, still holding on to the case, I finally asked her how, in what circumstances, was she certain . . .? She didn't answer my questions immediately, simple as they were.

'Shame, shame, I was so ashamed . . . I've never been so ashamed . . . and I'll never be so ashamed ever again . . .'

'But what of? It was for him to be ashamed, wasn't it? Be reasonable, Klara—it was for him to be ashamed, do you hear, not you!'

Silence.

'You don't understand at all, do you? Back there, it was for me to be ashamed.'

'And did he see you?'

'No . . . he just walked by me with the others . . . he couldn't have recognised me anyway, but just the same I hung my head and tried to make myself inconspicuous—I was ashamed, not afraid, just so ashamed . . . He was there on a visit with other dignitaries. I thought it was Himmler, but I was told no, Himmler had been there once, but before I was in the camp . . . I didn't even know my father was in the S.S. He must have wangled it. With a Jewish ex-wife, he took refuge in the S.S. I have a very prudent father . . . handsome, too . . . still handsome as ever . . . very, very handsome. Cowards and swine can be handsome. That's one of the things you learn . . . and shame.'

She was agitated, and trying to control her conflicting emotions. I wanted to take her in my arms, or, failing that, to console her with words. Yes, last evening I felt that impulse again, but I merely sat there and neither said nor did anything. She makes such gestures impossible.

Afterwards the tension lessened. I asked her if she would have fired the gun at the children.

'No, of course not. You don't waste ammunition for a sunset. I'm ill, but I'm not crazy.'

She'd realised she'd been talking too freely, and no doubt sensing my disapproval, added, 'Not children, that's impossible.'

But did she say it just to reassure me?

It was two in the morning, and I stood up to go to my room. I was almost at the door when she asked me, 'Do you know how my mother died?'

It took me a few seconds to decide whether or not to tell the truth. I told the truth. I told her everything: the two rather dubious letters that both arrived at the same time, one announcing Margarethe's death, the other speaking of suicide, and what Rainer told me then about our mother's having provided the poison. Klara listened very closely, but her only comment was, 'Oh! so that was it . . .' I offered to look for the two letters, but she didn't want me to.

'*I* believe *you*, you see.'

I tried to tease her then. I always try to do that a bit, though admittedly less and less, in order to get back on to our old footing of complicity. Up till now with no success.

Just before we parted, Klara said, 'There was a camp near Weimar . . . my father was very keen on Goethe . . .'

I said, 'What would Goethe have thought of all those readers of Goethe?'

When he went to Auschwitz, Ullrich Adler was a senior

officer . . . I thought of my mother, who used to say: 'For him, loyalty to his ancestors took the place of intelligence and feeling.'

I've met Fabienne at last. I was afraid she might be over-bearing. But she's natural and uncomplicated. There's nothing excessive about her voice or behaviour. She has brown, extremely watchful eyes and a smile that reminds you of spring. Her voice smiles too. She's warm without being intrusive, firm without being stern. She inspires confidence at once because she doesn't seek it. I hope we'll go on meeting more often after Klara's gone. I don't want to start a relationship now, just through Klara.

She says she's going to leave, disappear, and we'll never see her again. Meanwhile, she's here. Meanwhile, she talks. Meanwhile, I'd also like a holiday from Klara. Her presence makes me feel old. She's wearing me out.

Of course, she's putting on a front, but there's so much hatred in what she says, and nothing at the moment to take its place. That's the opposite of prostration, and a sign of good health, Alban would say. Maybe so.

~

Hatred. I think I may risk using the word, forceful though it may be. If I'd considered the word in relation to myself, I'd have seen it as expressing itself passionately, with excess, shatteringly, with violence. An emotion that's visible, obvious. Instead of which, Klara's voice speaks calmly of soul-searing things that become cool as she speaks of them. Somehow, I don't know how, she manages to express her hatred coldly. Almost lightly. There's a permanent dichotomy between the horrible things she relates and the way she speaks of them.

With cynicism, chuckles, unrelenting laughter. You can't laugh with her.

Sometimes her impassive grey eyes seek mine. It's a mannerism, or rather a code that I've just managed to decipher in the last few days. I'm less shocked now by what she says, but I worry about the dose of cruelty she pours out on me drop by drop. The gentle Klara, with whom I used always to feel safe, is now insidiously corrosive. She's corroding me. And it hurts. The drop of acid produced by her undeclared hatred. I'm learning to understand what's between the words. Klara's killing me by inches. It's only now I'm beginning to realise it. But I'll hold out until she leaves. Yes, now I want her to go. I *want* her to go!

Agathe has just phoned. The latest news from Barbery is that Victoire's doll has been drowned. She was saved, but all the paint has been washed off her face. Victoire is thrilled and pretends she's the doctor. Antoine has got out his paint-brushes, and tonight he's going to bring the roses back to poor Mimi's cheeks. In the morning, Victoire will think it's a miracle, or else proof of her own medical skills! Lots of love, my pet!

I skip the preliminaries. Too lazy to find the place where I should pick up the thread again. The story is a path strewn with pebbles that one sets aside or pushes on further, things that you keep or reject according to your mood or inclination or need. Without knowing why, you suddenly stop. You recognise the place, decide to stay there, you don't care about the path any more, you won't go that way again, you'll go somewhere else, along other ways that also lead somewhere in the end. This method is easy but chaotic too. But that's how it is.

Klara: 'Not to be able to ignore reality, to be every moment at the centre of it. In normal life there are little opportunities to escape, vanishings, possibilities of flight, all kinds of distraction, your thoughts are free to wander. I can imagine a scene or remember a person while I'm washing a plate or having a bath . . . back there it was impossible. Reality and nothing but reality. For the first week I thought everything must be untrue . . . it must have been my happy childhood that let me refuse to accept what I was experiencing, and perhaps those few days of absolute refusal prepared me to endure the equally absolute conviction that there would never again be anything but this, which had always existed and always would. And this decision, which was not a decision but rather an unconscious determination, the causes of which I didn't analyse, to go on living in spite of everything, inside a kind of bubble or capsule, without asking myself questions, was an exact continuation of my childhood happiness, with exactly the same attitude of taking everything for granted. Being without hope yet not being in despair, that was the flimsy lifeline to which one had to cling.'

No, I'm wrong. Sometimes one goes over the whole scene in search of the lost thread, the lost path. Often one doesn't recognise it.

Klara: (tensely) 'In the camps there was a kind of two-way relationship between us and others, between victims and victimisers, the pleasure of being with others, you see, being there in relation to one another, and so on, side by side, and so on, concerned with the truth, concerned with something or other—apart from the private fact of our existence.

'Back there, all philosophies failed, all of them. A Nazi snare . . . not even our own.

'Those who've come back will always know what extremes are, all possible extremes, and even what lies between the extremes—all the nuances of Being. Hence, no more philosophy. Ever. As God has gone up in smoke, so has philosophy, all parts of it, ethics, aesthetics and so on, all of it—everything collapsed back there, nothing held out, so that's that. All political systems, however carefully constructed, well worked out and elegant, all the learned and hazy elucubrations, the crazy amateur efforts of naïve, infantile, pretentious maniacs—pooh, chuck 'em away! Clear the decks, all gone!

'But that doesn't fool me! I know there'll be others, that at this very moment, in their rooms, they're working out other philosophies, other systems, other explanations on the ruins of what's just happened, they'll go on jawing about Being and Non-Being, with as many capital letters and ejaculations (sic) as possible. They'll go on— talk, talk, talk, scribble, scribble, scribble. Sophists, loads of sophists under the patronage of Goebbels, the last of the philosophers, Saint Goebbels, practitioner of all philosophies, cook, murderer . . . nothing left but the private fact of our existence.'

'Philosophy's not to blame, Klara—it's what you do or don't do with it . . .'

She interrupts me.

'Then it's obscene. If no system of thought is strong enough to oppose twelve years of madness, if no philosophy permeates a society thoroughly enough to prevent it from sinking into obscenity, then it is obscene itself. Or else it should be made known that all these learned treatises are there just to make students' lives miserable and win notoriety . . . it's enough to make you laugh, really.'

~

Klara's constant hankering for laughter. As defence, liberation, pride. A temporary or final riposte.

I don't think there's any point in contradicting her. She's too angry, with those cold attacks of wrath that make her stiffen on her chair and look even paler and more feverish than usual, and make me afraid she's going to faint. She hides her hands under the table, but when she flicks the ash off her cigarette I can see they're shaking. She sees that I see, and that makes her more furious still, probably because she knows I won't say anything to prolong the argument. I've neither the strength nor the wish to do so: conversations that start like this always turn into a monologue, putting me into a position where I can only either acquiesce or raise objections.

To tell her that philosophy is above all an instrument of knowledge, an approach to and research into the why and how of things—she knows all that, anyway—to try to make her see that her point of view is too narrow, strikes me as useless.

She concludes by saying:

'The only thing you can say with certainty is that human beings are revoltingly tough. You *can* say that, and that's about all . . . though it's plenty . . .'

To make her stop gnawing at her philosophical bone, I ask:

'What about poetry, Klara, do you condemn that the way you do philosophy?'

This surprises her, I think; confuses her too. I can see she's gradually calming down. She tells me to wait, she's thinking, and wants to sort out her ideas. This is typical Klara—sorting things out. She needs to do it. I'm sure she's spontaneous basically, but I imagine she often plans ahead to talk about something from a particular angle; anyway, she thinks about it in advance. Instead of writing something down, she thinks about it in order to speak of it, to get rid of it. This isn't a set programme to be accomplished, just a path to follow in order to go on living. I realise it's important for her. We have to stick it out. *I* have to stick it out.

'Poetry, yes. But what is poetry? What is philosophy? Moments of poetry, pure gems, fragments of poetry, gathering like an oblation a shy sign of affection, an unexpected gentleness in a look, a pitying tear from someone as unhappy as you are, and the fact that it does you good, the clear laugh of a young girl who has not yet suffered disaster, the lovely face of a new prisoner, and that you can still see it, a dandelion flower, can still bend down and breathe in for a moment all the yellow splendour, draw strength from the yellow for another hour; a Slovak woman singing as she de-louses her friend one Sunday afternoon— you forget the setting, you shut your eyes, the voice is beautiful—to be able to hear it, to let yourself be steeped in it as if getting into a warm bath. Is that poetry? It has to be, to have such power and so many repercussions . . . or else poetry could be the ability to seize such numberless instants of grace, though one can capture only an infinitesimal few of them . . . as with the stars . . . that would be an exception to what I was talking about just now, an exception to the general inability to escape. No, the thread of poetry was not cut off in Oswiecim. Not for me. Even if it was only words. Lots of people kept saying names, rolled them round in their mouths, sometimes only words. It's enough to say yes or no, or a name, a word, and cling on to it firmly until it becomes a chain too . . . which can either strangle or save. I met a Frenchwoman who kept repeating to herself the word "velvet". I don't find it a very pretty word, but for her it was magnificent because it soothed her, reminded her of beauty, warmth, softness, festivity, perhaps splendour—all things that didn't exist in Oswiecim. She used to work in a theatre, as a dresser, I think. But velvet was never more velvety than in the camp. Perhaps the word saved her . . . or drove her mad. Is that poetry? . . . if so, then it was there too. Rare, brief moments it would be a pity to forget.'

Friday 31 Henri-Martin

Klara's on her own in the rue Richer. It was she who insisted on it.

When I told her Fabienne would be there tomorrow evening, she said, 'No, I must try being alone before I leave, and I'm starting today.'

Tomorrow evening we're meeting at Agathe's. Adrien's bringing the children. Alban, Agathe and Adrien were all in on it. They'd made sure Alban and Fabienne would be free. Adrien and the children are leaving again on Sunday morning. Antoine doesn't like being at Barbery without a car.

I'm looking forward to Saturday evening. We'll all sleep there overnight. Adeline's supplying the dinner, dessert included. It's a surprise! Agathe's all excited about the prospect of this dinner. She agrees to our inviting Fabienne.

Klara's leaving on Sunday the 9th. For London. Her ship leaves the following week—I've forgotten the date. I'm usually good at remembering dates. But I've forgotten the date when Klara's ship sails.

We've known it for a week. But I didn't want to think about it.

She's arranging her affairs with Léandre, meeting him in the lawyer's office or in a café. She'll sign separately for the sale of her apartment. Antoine will sign too. A bank account has been opened in New York. She won't have any immediate financial problems. Everything depends on the lifestyle she chooses to adopt.

I write coldly about these practical matters—they bore me because my mind is on other things. What really worries me is how I'm going to get used to this break, and to regard it as final, as she's often told us it will be. I find this unthinkable, more cruel than her actual death would be. Shall I be able to reconcile her absence and my knowledge that she's still alive?

Alban has reminded me that half the apartment in the rue Richer belongs to Rainer, and thus to Klara, his widow. (It's incongruous, but officially she *is* a widow, widow Roth as far as her administrative status is concerned, though the words are crude, insensitive, at the same time true and false. 'Widow Roth' doesn't mean anything.)

We talked about it this afternoon. Klara was quite determined. She doesn't want to inherit anything from Rainer. She regards herself as divorced, not widowed. She's told me so several times. She doesn't spare me anything.

'There are limits to the concessions one can make. I'm taking what my mother gave me—I need it just to get started in America, with a photo lab or something. I want to have a modicum of independence at first, and then we'll see. I shan't stay on in New York, I'd prefer somewhere warmer, so I'll go further south, Mexico perhaps . . . I'll think about it over there.'

While she was about it, she informed me she was going to change her name.

'A common English first name, like Mary, and a very common surname—the name of a number, for instance, something that will always be above suspicion.'

This was probably intended to make me laugh.

' "Twenty-two" wouldn't be bad, or "double-something" . . . "carbon copy?"—no! Something simpler, very simple, I was only joking . . .'

This is something new. But it doesn't make me laugh. I remember how Rainer and I used to sing the *Winterreise*.

> *Was vermeid ich denn die Wege*
> *Wo die andern Wandrer gehn?*

> *Hab ja doch nichts begangen*
> *Dass ich die Menschen sollte schen!*

> *Welch ein törichtes Verlangen*
> *treibt mich in die Wüstenein?*

> [Why do I avoid the paths
> Followed by other travellers?

I have done nothing
To make me flee mankind!

What mad compulsion
Drives me towards the wilderness?]

Afterwards, to cheer us up, he would improvise dance-tunes, to words like, 'It's better than Putzi, it's better than Putzi . . .'

When Klara asked him in Russian, 'Rainer, play us something sad,' he would wander at length through the Nocturnes of Chopin, his favourites. Christmas '41. That was the last time. The last time Rainer played the piano for us.

It's impossible not to talk about Victoire before Klara leaves. This makes me feel quite ill.

A few days ago, a week perhaps, I can't say, Klara spoke about Sundays in the camps. One scene:

A group of women huddled round a bit of mirror, passing it from one to another. Suddenly, shouting broke out and one of the women hurled the glass away, yelling, 'What's the matter with this mirror?' Then there was laughter, some cruel, some embarrassed.

'A lot of us wouldn't believe what we saw in the mirror!' said Klara calmly.

Saturday, September 1, 1945 Henri-Martin

Midday. I just phoned Klara. She hadn't had a good night, but better than she'd expected. She thinks she'll be able to carry on. She asked if it would be possible for the three of us to meet during the coming week. 'There's not much time left.'

I said, 'We'll talk about Victoire.' It was a statement. 'Yes, certainly,' she answered at once.

Phew! That's a relief.

Left Agathe at the beginning of the afternoon. Adrien and the children have gone back to Barbery. Yesterday evening was exciting, reinvigorating, magnificent, gay, amusing, affectionate, gentle—all at once.

At one point I wept—it was too much for me. I thought my heart would burst. My tears helped me calm down. I was ashamed, but I couldn't stop. I haven't cried for a long time. Alban put his arms round me and comforted me as if I were a child. 'We've had to be too strong for too long, so of course we eventually break down,' he said.

And then came tears of joy to mix with the sadness, because without any warning Rainer passed through the room. I had a vision of Rainer. It's all a bit confused in my mind because I think I started to cry before he appeared, in which case it was the tears that made him come.

Fortunately the children were in bed. They wouldn't have understood.

They're in splendid form, with cheeks like peaches and the rest of their bodies caramel-coloured. Agathe has made

143

them some baggy shorts out of odd bits of material, grey in front and black behind, with red shoulder-straps, brightened up further with two round, red, hip pockets like rosy cheeks. The kids have learned to romp in a way that invites the rosy cheeks to be smacked. They can sing *Frère Jacques* and *Meunier tu dors*. They're so proud of themselves! Antoine is getting them both to learn the piano. 'We play meesic,' said Isidore solemnly. Anyhow, the fresh air quietens them down; at nine o'clock they go off to bed without a murmur.

Pâté, *lapin chasseur*, plum tart. Adeline spoils us.

Another surprise was Henry, whom we didn't know. He's a friend of Adrien's, but older, and if I understood some of their allusions right, he was in the same resistance group. He's very discreet, but it didn't escape my notice that several times he went and found various utensils from the kitchen without any difficulty . . . Agathe didn't say anything to me today; she's probably waiting—yesterday evening was a turning point. Perhaps we'll see the feline, enigmatic Henry again. I hope so with all my heart, for Agathe's sake.

I nearly forgot to mention he has only one hand. So at the table there was one person with an eye missing, another with only one arm, plus two orphans, plus Agathe without Frédéric, plus me without Rainer, plus Klara . . . We'll go on living without, or we'll go on living with. No more war, no more war, no more war ever.

Adrien's going to try to get in to Sciences-Po. Imagine Adrien as a diplomat!

The war was a determining factor in his choice. We've talked about it a lot.

Fabienne couldn't come.

Klara's taking one of the big suitcases from the rue Lafayette with her when she leaves.

She's taking two Leicas, the Rolleiflex, the Ciné-Kodak and the Kodascope, the super-Ikonta and the Rétina, leaving us one Leica and the Pathé-Baby.

This morning: Klara was talking about the political and racial deportees. The 'r' grates deep in her throat.

'They won't all be able to talk as I've been able to, here with you.' (Is this a thank-you? *Hoffentlich ja.*) 'They'll go back silently to what they were doing before. If they can. Being a torturer was a profession, being a victim is not. The prisoners of war and the politicals will return to what they were doing before. Especially the politicals.

'It was only in Cracow I found out that some of them were in touch with the Polish resistance . . . they didn't tell me themselves . . . didn't think me worthy of their confidence . . . in my last position I could have done something, passed on information, what I saw and heard might have been useful, I was pretty smart, and still fit enough to be efficient . . . if I had joined in I'd have been justified in doing so . . . but instead . . . I went to the extreme of stupidity and humiliation. The four girls who were hanged in January had been helping the resistance . . .

'I didn't have the chance to choose . . . but I wonder . . . if I had had the choice . . . I mean, like any German . . . would I have been able to react properly, otherwise it's impossible to answer the question . . . But is it the right question? Anyway, it *is* a question . . . and one that requires an answer. In the absence of an answer, the question remains, it exists, and so does the answer; even if it takes time to find it, the answer has to be there . . . perhaps one has to put up with a hypothetical answer until one can muster the courage to give a lucid, true one.

'There were some Frenchwomen who were political prisoners, about a hundred of them . . . a solid mass. At first they kept saying, "We're French politicals, we're French politicals" . . . which meant "*We*'re not racial prisoners, *we*'re here for good reason." A claim to be a kind of aristocracy, as against the common herd. They could have said the same to the children—"We're French political prisoners, French political prisoners, not children." Another class of person, if not another species. I tried to make contact with them. I felt like a beggar. But as a German and not a communist, I hadn't a chance. Perhaps the best of them felt sorry for me . . . yes, I could see some did, but their pity was so sickening it made you want to run a mile.'

In June, at the Lutétia, in the space of a couple of days, I'd had the opportunity to talk to two women back from

Auschwitz, both French politicals, one from Paris, the other from the provinces. One of them was quite refined, the other rather uncouth. Neither did more than glance at my photographs of Klara. I knew it was useless. But like everyone else I was clumsy and asking too much. I kept asking them questions, they kept shaking their heads, obviously trying to pay attention, but either not answering or telling me things that were beside the point.

The refined one: 'I don't want to give you false hopes. There's not much chance of her coming back, especially if she's Jewish. I'm very sorry to have to say so, madame, but you'd better be prepared . . .' Then she added gently, as if by way of consolation, 'Perhaps it's for the best, you know.' That was all.

The uncouth one: 'Jewish? Sent there in '42? Forget it.'

And like the other one, she said no more.

I said to Klara: 'But they suffered too, you know. Paid dear for their activities, I believe. Only a few of them came back.'

Klara: 'Yes, but they knew why, and made sure we knew too . . . Overdid it.'

I remember all those people arriving at the Lutétia. I had reservations about showing the photographs. I knew it was pointless. In the case of recent deportees or prisoners of war, pictures might help, but not for the others, they were all unrecognisable by now, as we soon realised. All those people intimidated me, I was nervous about approaching them, I could see that every question either wearied or wounded them. You couldn't regard them as ordinary invalids. Some of the volunteer workers were too heavy-handed in their efforts to help; the patronising attitude of certain do-gooders was insufferable. The two women who'd been in Auschwitz had come from Ravensbrück via Oslo. They seemed lost, so fragile, on the brink of something—a fainting fit, hysterics or weeping, physical collapse. Anything was possible. Several times I asked them to forgive me. I no longer knew what to do to or say to protect them from my questions.

Alban found himself in the same quandary, but he was helped by his position as a doctor, which was a little more acceptable. Not always, though.

At the Lutétia, I was upset by the blunders, the incomprehension, the gaffes and mistakes committed on all sides. I wasn't the only person to suffer such embarrassments. I arranged to be on duty less often, then stopped going altogether.

Administrative questions met with rebellion, resentment or resignation. It was the last that floored me. I tried to be as tactful as possible, but I couldn't change the nature of the questions, and it was the questions themselves that were upsetting. Many of those I dealt with had no clear memory of dates, places or the order of events. Some people got confused, others couldn't remember anything at all. Some made pathetic efforts to oblige, some clammed up sulkily or just wilted. Others were aggressive or seemed frightened. For all of them the questionnaires were an ordeal. You could see that all they wanted was sleep, rest, medical attention, some kindness if possible.

Naturally, all this had nothing in common with Klara's arrogance after five months of wandering. The uneasiness one feels with her is quite different, harsher. Her self-assurance, her haughtiness preserve her from pity. I must admit I prefer her attitude.

Tuesday 4 Rue Richer, Evening

The count-down; only four days left. A kind of anguish.

Klara seems light-hearted, as if the imminence of her departure lent her wings.

For the first time, she asked me questions.

'What was the war like for you after I went away?'

I said nothing about this apartment—how it was used as a safe house, a 'letter-box', a store for compromising papers, being apparently closed up, though seldom empty; I said nothing about Rainer's last visit, his silence, his despair, his decision to fight; nothing about Alban at the hospital and the people camouflaged as patients; nothing about our activities *before* she went away—we never referred to any of that in front of her. After July '42 I was much more careful; I was afraid for Victoire. I didn't want her to find herself alone. What would have been the use of talking about all that?

I just mentioned the arrests we heard of, the shooting of hostages, the air-raids in the year before the Liberation of Paris, the restrictions that were in force even before '42 and that got worse later, the role of the F.T.P. [Francs-tireurs et Partisans] and the F.F.I. [Forces Françaises de l'Intérieur], the demonstrations in July '44 and the strikes that followed, the French flag on the Eiffel Tower, the 2nd Armoured Division on August 25th, the liberation of the Majestic in the afternoon, the barricades, the Americans on the 28th, the fire at the Grand Palais, the departure of the Germans, the wounded, the dead—more than a thousand according to Alban, and many more on the German side, apparently. I told her how afraid I was of being arrested even though my papers were in order, my fears about the concierge at the rue Henri-Martin, a snooper known to be a denouncer of Jews. Alban was careful to pay her properly for whatever she did—the slightest irregularity might arouse her suspicion and put us in danger. Despite my disgust, I managed to be pleasant to her. Painful as it was to stoop so low, it was necessary in order to protect us all.

We arranged for all three of us to meet on the Thursday evening.

Klara wanted it to be here. She would see to the dinner . . . !

I'm to be with her all day on Saturday. On Friday she'll see Fabienne. On Sunday it will be all over.

I went to the dinner in an uneasy frame of mind, determined that all that had to be said should be said calmly. It went off with as little trouble as possible. Some emotion, some tensions were inevitable, but we did come to an agreement.

I hope to God it's not a bad one.

Alban and I had worked out a plan. Whatever happened, we wouldn't conceal from Victoire the existence of her natural parents. As far as Rainer is concerned there was no problem, but that still left us with the question of Klara. Wishing to respect her decision, we proposed either to suggest that she had disappeared, though without excluding the possibility that she might re-appear, or else to explain that she was unable, temporarily or permanently, to take care of Victoire herself. Explanations, we said, could be gone into if and when Victoire asked questions. As time went by, we could, using the truth as our basis, supply details of circumstances and fill out her knowledge. We'd suggest that Klara might reverse her decision in a few years' time, and want to

153

resume relations with us and with her daughter, and that, depending on the circumstances then, it could probably be done without too much upset. To us this plan seemed feasible, and the least awkward solution for Klara, Victoire, and ourselves.

Alban and I took it in turns to put our point of view to Klara as advantageously as possible.

She heard us out without interrupting. When we'd finished, there was a long but not uncomfortable silence. Then:

'You forget that I died at Brzezinka.

'You forget that I'll never come back to Europe.

'You forget that I'm going to change my name. I'm going to disappear. Klara Schwartz-Adler is going to disappear.

'It's easy to tell the child your father died a hero's death and your mother died in Poland. It's the truth.

'I can tell you what it would be like for this little girl if I were to take her back. We can examine the case together. Imagine me coming back here to claim her from you. You couldn't deny I had the right, even though she's declared in your names. But without your agreement and no doubt a lot of legal procedures I couldn't take her away with me. And supposing I did, supposing I kidnapped her, because that's what it would be, if I wanted at all costs to have the child I gave birth to three years ago, whom I didn't declare, whom I didn't even nurse . . . it would be two people unknown to one another going off to America far away from you. Because I'd still insist on a total break with

Europe . . . and with you. Imagine the child, the child you know now. Imagine what she'll be like in six months. She won't speak French any more, and she won't speak English yet, she won't be able to laugh any more, though maybe she'll still cry, her hair will be cut short . . . She's never known anything about the war, and she'll learn about it from someone who's ill. Understand what I'm saying—I'm an unexploded mine. A bomb that could explode at any moment. For me to take her back would be to push her into a minefield. It'll take time to defuse everything, time that will destroy a little girl's childhood, a whole childhood swallowed up by that permanent danger. The danger I represent, the danger of Oswiecim.

'Inside, I'm just dead, I taste of death, I reek of it, and shall do for a long time, perhaps for ever. Children sense it. I don't want her to get a whiff of that smell, which she hasn't yet experienced. *We*, you and I, had happy childhoods. Why shouldn't she? With me, she wouldn't escape Brzezinka. She's been spared it so far—why inflict its aftermath on her?'

Alban: 'There's never been any question of abandoning Victoire to you. We could have found a compromise, but that would have meant you staying on here . . . Lika and I . . .'

Klara: 'You are her parents, I know. I feel it. Believe me or not as you like, but I tell you that has made me a bit happy, a bit calm, from the start. I don't know exactly why I came back here, but that's what has made the journey worthwhile. Try to understand. I'm not rejecting my daughter. It's myself I'm rejecting, casting myself out of her life for the sake of her life. I have nothing to give her but my pain and my madness, my illness, for that's what it is—I'm ill, and not likely to get better soon . . . It would be wrong-headed to suggest that the child might cure me . . . that's not what a child, and its one brief childhood, is for. It has other things to do.'

I said: 'We've never had that idea, Klara. Everything you say is quite clear and has been understood by us ever since you came back. But it doesn't explain why, knowing what we know, we should tell Victoire you are dead . . .'

Klara: 'Because, from the beginning, we've spoken of only one thing. Abandonment. I know you don't misunderstand. From the start we've talked only of that . . . abandonment . . . who abandons whom. In the case I've been describing, it would be you who would be doing the abandoning. In my own case, it would be I who was abandoning her . . . if I were alive. If I'm dead, she isn't abandoned at all. And that's what I want.'

Alban: 'There are some things a child understands. As Lika said, an explanation given gradually, over time . . .'

Klara: 'No. You don't know what abandonment is. A child dies of it. I know. Only too well. Believe me, I know. I implore you to believe me . . .'

That 'I implore you' silenced and alerted us dramatically. Its effect was strange, disturbing, it commanded respect. Now Alban and I both knew how grave the situation really was. We were forced to drop our own point of view because there had emerged a force and a knowledge greater than ours, a pain, hitherto hidden, about to be revealed. Our long closeness to Klara gave us a presentiment of what was to come.

Alban, almost inaudibly: 'Say what you have to say, Klara. Say it now.'

Klara: 'Yes.'

Silence. A long silence.

She sat back in her chair, rested her forearms on the table, spread her hands out flat. We all—together, I'm sure—took a deep breath.

Throughout the story Klara was to tell us, she would close her eyes, open them, be back in the camps, as if back in the camps; she'd look at the wall, or at Alban or me, and she'd look beautiful, beautiful, Klara beautiful again at last. Her voice was still harsh, but now harmonious too.

I'm profoundly moved as I try to remember accurately and in detail the story of little Ulli.

'Back there I had a child, a little boy. I mean . . . he appeared there one day in our hut, no one knew how, no one ever found out. It was at the end of November last year. They'd stopped gassing people.

'A little boy who'd been loved. He wasn't even thin, or dirty, or in rags. Someone who cared very much must have seen that he was properly fed. Perhaps they'd seen to it that he laughed, too. There was evidence about the food. Not about the laughter. He was very serious. He never laughed.

Or cried. But his face was open, his eyes were not vague, not dead, not frightened, not mistrustful, not unintelligent. They were watchful. He never spoke, but he wasn't dumb, not physically. Once, just once, he said no to a woman; he said it in German. He wasn't deaf, either. When I sang him songs in German and Russian he beat time with his fingers on the palm of my hand or on my thigh. For he was mine. I was the first to give him a name, and then the others gave up and said he was mine . . . but *he* had chosen *me* first. When I held his hand, he let me. When the others did it, he took his hand away . . . not quickly or roughly, but firmly, as he did everything. All the other women gave him food through me; he would take it from me. They all accepted the situation . . . at least, they all helped to hide him, watch over him, ward off danger. We were all accomplices in this, even the guard in charge of the block—yes, that happened there, in the hell of Brzezinka, a child could live, go on living . . . with women . . . with me . . . he slept beside me . . . During the day, I used to sneak away to be with him, talk to him, tell him stories, but above all to talk to him a lot . . . I used to talk to him about the end of the war, and how we'd soon be free, and go away, and how everything would be better, and that I wouldn't leave him, and perhaps we might find his mother, and then perhaps he'd speak, but I understood his silence now, and didn't ask him to speak; as often as possible I called him by the name I'd given him . . .'

I asked: 'Please, Klara, what name did you give him?'

Klara, without hesitation: 'I called him Ulli. Ulli is the name I gave him . . . I talked to him about his mother, and his father, but mostly his mother, and that perhaps we'd find her, and then he'd go away with her when the war was over. I told him his mother hadn't been able to do otherwise, that she was sure to be nice, that perhaps she was ill and perhaps she was dead, and one day he'd talk about her, but only when he wanted to. When I talked to him about his mother, he clutched my hand tighter, he had large hands, still chubby; when I mentioned his mother, he pressed his fingers into my hand . . . that's all . . . I used to say you'll see, you'll see, Ulli, we'll both look for your mother, I promise you, when the other soldiers come, the nice soldiers, they'll come soon, people will ask a lot of questions, and perhaps you'll ask some questions too, and if we don't find her we'll go to a family some distance from here, I promise you, with other children smaller than you, who haven't been through the war like you, and you'll be the biggest, you'll be big and everyone will love you, I told him . . . I told him . . . lots of the things you tell a little boy who's inconsolable.

'I used to talk to him in German. At first, we tried all the languages that were spoken in the hut, but it was German he understood. Perhaps he was Czech or German . . . I kept talking and talking to him so that he'd believe me, believe as strongly as I did, I believed so firmly, in November we began to believe, and Ulli helped me to believe even more. Probably I talked so much in order that he should believe me, or that's what I thought afterwards, in order that he should believe in all the things I said . . . possible, reasonable things, within our reach, credible for a young child . . .

pretty things too, I thought of everything, even that, pretty things to say . . . yes.'

Klara was silent for a long time.

Alban sat with his head in his hands.

I had a lump in my throat. Of course we knew what was coming.

But it had to be said.

Klara didn't move. She looked beautiful; her features were softened.

She was calm. We got up to have a drink of water.

In silence.

We moved cautiously, almost ceremoniously, Alban and I.

Klara's eyes followed us. She was waiting.

We knew what the end would be. We were already performing the ritual.

'One evening I came back to the block. Some silences are special; they cry out to you. The combination of all the other women's silences that evening, together with the way they avoided me, told me everything in a few seconds. Ulli was stretched out on my mattress. Dead. His eyes open. Dead . . . I went close to him and said, "You were right, Ulli." There was no one to contradict me . . . I stood there, my eyes overflowing with tears, but without a sob, my eyes open gazing at Ulli, his eyes open too. For Ulli, no weeping, just tears flowing like water from a tap, the last water I had in my body. After the death of my last girl friend, I didn't even know I had any left. My tear glands now are nothing but little raisins, all wrinkled and dry.

'That's Oswiecim: knowing when, where and why you've laughed for the last time; when, where and why you've wept for the last time; knowing that both those natural functions have been destroyed; having other occasions for them, but realising that laughter and tears are no longer possible, and remembering the circumstances of the last time. There—you leave things like that behind you at Oswiecim. That's what Oswiecim is like . . .

'It's a place that is dry, though it's full of mud—it has dried up everything else. There was no gas chamber for Ulli, yet he was burned up, like the others, and like my last tears.

'It was the twentieth of last December. Five weeks later, the Russians were there.

'The dead have their reasons.

'Ulli could have lived. He lacked for nothing during the three weeks he was with us. Yet without being ill or neglected, he died. He decided to die. In such a young child, a refusal. He didn't believe us, any of us; he didn't believe me. An eternal doubt, or rather no longer doubt, but total disbelief, disbelief towards a world that steals mothers and creates enormous sorrow. He preferred not to go through all that.

'If I'd told you the story as it really was, it would have taken me only another two weeks or a month to throw myself on the barbed-wire when Ulli died. He was in a hurry, I think. He didn't wait for me to be a possible mother for him, I hadn't managed to convince him. That would call for a love of exceptional power, no doubt. But I was poor. I gave and gave, and then I scrabbled about for crumbs, but presumably even so I didn't have much, anyhow not enough to hold back a little boy. And now I have nothing left.

'My last particles of love were for noble little Ulli, who died for the best possible reason—refusing to live beyond acceptable limits. All those who came back went far beyond those limits. Nothing to boast of in that.'

'One might take the opposite view,' I said.

Klara: 'I didn't throw myself against the barbed-wire. He was right not to believe me . . .

'Perhaps Ulli absented himself so that the questions should remain. Unless his death is an answer we haven't dared listen to. Die, die, why don't you? Perhaps that's what he was saying, but, as you may imagine, no one wants to hear it, especially in a place like that!

'That's why we ought to kill all the torturers, to make sure that memory doesn't survive, doesn't lie putrefying in some brain or other. We ought to kill them so that it's impossible for a human race that has so demeaned the human race to go on living as if nothing had happened. The worst thing for humanity is that people should live who have put themselves outside humanity. Yes, I would kill them. Not for revenge; no. Just for hygienic reasons, the health of the world. But also in memory of the ignominy that made us accomplices in order to survive, the ignominy that besmirched and contaminated us, tattooed our very souls—that should also be wiped out so as to destroy any traces of it. And *we* ought to be killed too, the victims ought to be killed too. But I know . . . the Nazis slaughtered in the name of *their* sort of hygiene . . . so let's not do anything, though the world is the worse for.'

It was a long monologue. Klara didn't move, her hands were still lying flat. She didn't smoke or drink. She was telling the story of little Ulli, she needed nothing else. We too sat motionless, our eyes on Klara.

'Ulli said more than no—he said a superlative of no. A word that doesn't exist. A total no, and one that's not a yes to something else. Perhaps the word doesn't exist in any language because those who convey its meaning don't bother to express it in language, don't linger on earth to formulate the one word common to them all, the word of all those who die because of that more than no or otherwise than no. Only they could invent it, but that doesn't interest them, they are simply *in* that word that doesn't exist and that we can't say for them; otherwise . . . All that's left is regret, and the shame of not being one of them.'

Long silence.

'Perhaps a child doesn't commit suicide. He makes his heart stop, that's all. He has that power.

'The woman doctor from Warsaw told me Ulli must have had heart trouble. A medical verdict! I said yes, he had something wrong with his heart. I knew the symptoms. A child who doesn't laugh, doesn't cry, and doesn't speak for three weeks certainly has heart trouble. The woman was pleasant and sensitive. She said, "I give you a doctor's diagnosis, but I know what you think, and you're probably right."

'Ulli was right too.

'And for not seeing anyone again here, apart from you, I too had my reasons. Like the dead.

'If I'd come back with Ulli, I'd have brought up two children. With your help, I think—I'm sure—I'd have done it. But Europe is also the place of my defeat, the place where I was drained of everything. My story is part of the whole, larger scene. Within the great débâcle, I had a débâcle of my own.

'I don't want to endure any more of that strange suffering which consists in suffering from seeing others suffer.'

Silence.

'Now I'm left orphaned by that child.'

'Only by him?' I said.

Silence.

'Not only by him . . . I can't be a mother to any other child either.'

We went on talking for a long time. We weren't entirely convinced—especially Alban—but we bowed to her arguments and gave in.

When the time comes, we'll tell Victoire that her mother died in Auschwitz, in Upper Silesia, Poland.

It's six o'clock and I've been writing all day. In a little while, we're going out to a restaurant, Alban and I! I'm spending tomorrow with Klara. On Sunday afternoon at three o'clock we're taking her to the station. Today she's with Fabienne.

Tuesday, September 11, 1945

Klara has gone. Klara, Klara. So . . .

Brave Klara. I'm in mourning. Feeling at the same time bereft and yet not bereft.

On the platform she hugged me tight.

The last thing she did was wipe the tears from my face. A gentle gesture. As in the old days.

'Everything's been fine, everything will be all right.'

She got into the train before the whistle blew.

We left straight away.

I've been crying ever since. Such a huge void.

She said some good things during the last days:

'We've come a long way together, we three.'

'My corpses are still all there, and as numerous as ever, but thanks to you they're not so heavy. I'm beginning to stand up straight again.'

'Not many people could listen to all I've told you.'

'I haven't spared you. But if it was too tiring you haven't shown it.'

'You're brave, both of you. And gracious.'

'Now get some rest.'

'This month with you has been a great gift to me.'

And to me, as a kind of compliment:

'*You* would have thrown yourself on the barbed-wire.'

As a kind of injunction, referring to Victoire:

'I hope she laughs a lot!'

And later:

'I hope *your* children laugh a lot too!'

In this way she smuggled little snatches of thanks into her summing-up.

It's absurd. Right up to the last moment I hoped for a change of mind. The way she'd grown milder made me think it possible. Despite what I know, despite her last confidences on Saturday, I hoped with all my might for a last-minute volte-face. But as we talked, as if she guessed my ridiculous hope, she kept trying to put me right by throwing in such correctives as 'I have no regrets' and similar pointers.

Her big suitcase had been sent on in advance. She left with Margarethe's handsome little overnight bag. I found the little red attaché-case, all broken to pieces, in the dustbin. No trace of the coat from Cracow that looked like a dog.

Thursday, September 13, 1945 Henri-Martin

About Saturday.

Klara told me how the Reich was riddled with camps like holes in a cheese. Germany's future *trous de mémoire* [lapses of memory], she said.

She told me more about Berlin, its ruins, its columns of smoke, its stupefied ghosts, its tanks, its cars overturned like tortoises lying on their backs and not yet towed away, its lift-shafts standing alone with nothing around them, making you think of them, she said, as coffins for another kind of ascent, its cellars, its rats—Berlin and its splendours flattened, broken up into a kind of jigsaw-puzzle. Klara couldn't find her way, passed easily from one zone to another, always with the idea of finding the block of flats where her mother had lived. One week she finally found it, unscathed. A whole section of the street had been spared—she couldn't believe her eyes.

I'll do my best to reconstruct what followed.

She apparently knocked or rang at the door. Perhaps there

were chimes. The people opened the door. She said, 'I'm Klara Schwartz-Adler.' To avoid embarrassment, they looked astonished. 'Oh, we wouldn't have recognised you.' Later, in the hall, they were all the more nervous because they didn't want to show it. Imagine Klara's eyes drilling into their backs. In the dining-room they sat down—they'd just been finishing a meal. She remained standing. As she said, she was standing: they were seated. So embarrassed they didn't even invite her to join them. Or perhaps they did. She didn't say. So there was Klara, standing at the end of the table, the others seated. Settled comfortably into their chairs? Not settled comfortably into their chairs? She didn't say. Biedermeier table and chairs. 'Biedermeier table and chairs that had belonged to my grandmother,' she said with a wry laugh.

Imagine the effort they made to appear normal. The end of a meal. Frugal? Lavish? We don't know. This detail wasn't revealed. A conversation began at once, feverish on their side, curt and factual on hers. Imagine. Klara as we know her now, just the same, except perhaps harsher in that month of June in Berlin. The weather was fine then, she told us.

Three weeks in Berlin after Dresden, Linz, Prague, Cracow—Berlin a compulsory stop, a funerary stop. Berlin and its eight photographs.

Among others.

He or she: 'We wouldn't have recognised you . . . You've

changed . . . You were pretty in '38. Still, we've all had our troubles, haven't we?

'When you left in '38, with a Jew, I think, your mother was very unhappy, no doubt about it. In September '41—it was in September, wasn't it?—she ought to have worn the special badge, but well, your father probably protected her, didn't he? But we don't know about that. Anyhow, one day no one had seen her for a couple of days, and there was no sound from in here, so we called the police to break down the door. As you know, she'd killed herself, shot herself, in the other drawing-room, the little modern one . . . you couldn't get hold of any poison then, could you? So she shot herself . . .'

Klara: 'No, that's not true.'

She or he: 'You can always ask. If the records have survived, it's all written down. We tried to do the best we could for her, and believe me it was risky for us then, with Wolfgang and Gottlieb in the Wehrmacht, and Marcus too, Gertrude enlisted and Gisela—you remember Gisela, you played with her often enough, well, she's got four children now, so it was risky, very risky, you know—everything was risky then because of the Jews.'

Klara: 'No, because of the Nazis.'

The other two: 'Have it your own way, but if it hadn't been for the Jews there wouldn't have been any problem. The fact remains, we did the best we could for her. You have to remember the circumstances, Klara—we suffered too, suffered a lot. We lost a nephew on the Eastern Front, and a young cousin, an uncle, an aunt in the bombing of

Dresden—those raids were savage, barbaric, you don't know. Both our fathers died too . . .'

Klara: 'In their beds.'

The others: 'Yes, but they're dead just the same, Klara— death is death for everyone.'

Klara: 'So you're orphans.'

They: 'Don't take it like that, Klara . . . Yes, of course, in a way it's always hard to lose one's father at any age, you must know that yourself.'

Klara: 'I don't know if they die in the SS.'

And then? What happened afterwards? So far it had been just preliminaries, not very amiable, it's true, but just beating about the bush as if this was a mere courtesy call. Waiting, they were waiting for the question that was bound to fall on to their plates. They weren't going to broach the subject, said Klara, it was up to her.

'And what about the apartment?'

They: 'We managed to sort it out. That wasn't easy, either. Everything, everything was difficult. But all the same we did manage to buy it. For Gisela and Marcus and their four children, you see. It was far too big for just one person, everyone thought it was odd. Up till '41, it was incredible, especially in her situation. Your father must have protected her, there's no other explanation. Our Gisela had only five rooms. And you see, Klara, we need our own apartment too when the children come.'

~

Klara paused to remind me about Gisela. 'She was as dark as I was fair. A real Aryan,' said Klara derisively. 'After '35, she didn't speak to me any more, but she wasn't bad, just shy, and we steered clear of one another to avoid embarrassment.'

Personally, I don't remember the girl at all. Klara preferred to come to our place, so I couldn't have met Gisela often.

Klara: 'And the furniture? Did you buy that as well as the apartment?'

They: 'Where were we to put it? It was really to protect the furniture that we bought it and the flat together. Don't you worry, it was all included in the price.'

Klara: 'You have proofs, I presume.'

They: 'Yes, of course, we'll show you the papers.'

'She went and searched through Mother's desk, in Mother's bedroom,' said Klara. 'I recognised the sound. I thought I'd fall down in a faint, as they say in French. I must have given them a fright, because they said, "Do sit down, Klara," but I stuck it out. I asked them to show me the contract covering the sale. I read almost all of it, but remember nothing. It was very long. I can't recall the price, but even to me, who knows nothing about these things, it seemed ridiculously low. I said, "You're lying—an eight-room apartment, furnished, for the price of one room—that's impossible. You may well have helped my mother, your good neighbour, but your good neighbour was a good bargain for you, wasn't she?"'

They: 'Don't get worked up, Klara. Of course it wasn't expensive, but it was difficult to manage, especially then, and the papers don't show the compensation tax we had to pay. You're getting excited, but we're decent, honest people. After all, it's better that we should have the apartment rather than others; we knew you, it's not as if it were strangers, and we haven't changed anything, as you see.'

Klara: 'Have you got the paper about the compensation tax?'

They hesitated then, and the woman went back to Margarethe's room. 'I heard the sound of the desk again,' said Klara. 'She stayed there about ten minutes, during which he kept saying how well it had turned out in the end really, for them and for her. He wanted us to be friends. He went on chattering.'

'You knew Fräulein Kuntz, didn't you—she lives all on her own upstairs, deafer than ever—you remember Fräulein Kuntz? Apart from her, we're the only ones left. Gisela's taken her children to our house in the mountains, it's safer for her, she was right to go. The air-raids were terrible, we only survived by a miracle, but it was best to stay here because of the looting. We'd planned ahead, the cellar has been fitted up nicely—we can show you if you like, you won't recognise it. You did know the cellar?'

Klara said, 'I know all the cellars.'

He must have realised, then at least, that Klara wasn't going to play along with them.

When the woman came back empty-handed, she said, 'I shan't go on looking while you're here, but don't worry, we'll find it.'

Later still.

They: 'Calm down, Klara, anyway everything is in order. The law is on our side, whether you like it or not, and they're not going to change the law now. That was the price at the time, neither more nor less, and there's nothing you can do about it. Now, if you want to buy it back, we can talk about it, only you'll have to expect a readjustment—times are still hard, and as you may imagine, prices are soaring because of the housing shortage. But we can always come to some arrangement, Klara . . . We knew you when you were a little girl, and your poor mother, and . . .'

Klara: 'Times change enough to send prices up, but not enough to justify theft, because that's what we're talking about. As you were in a good position to know in the Ministry of Finance.'

They: 'No, no. And who was the victim of the theft, Klara? The State. It had all become the property of the State. You've forgotten all that—you weren't here, we didn't know how to get in touch with you, you were living peacefully in France, while we . . . our two sons and our son-in-law were in the army, it wasn't easy, and then there was Gisela and her four children. So you see how it was, and our sons had children too—you have to think things out, Klara, not look at everything from just one point of view.'

Klara: 'You might at least have the decency to offer me the difference between the real value and what you paid. That's the least you could do. Instead of which you want to sell me my own apartment for as much as you can get.'

They: 'Don't take on like that, Klara! You're getting it all wrong. All we say and all we've done has been perfectly correct—correct, do you hear? We haven't, like lots of other people, engaged in sharp practice. Everything was done according to the rules, you can be sure of that. But what's done is done, duly paid and signed for . . . And you must have property in France, judging by your poor mother. She was so careful and all, she won't have left you with nothing. And from what you said, you still have your father, haven't you?—he could help you . . .'

Klara: 'You know where I've come from.'

They: 'No, but from the look of you you must have had a hard time, like us . . .'

Klara: 'Oswiecim, you must have heard of it.'

They: 'No . . . In Poland?'

Klara told them the German name. They looked a little embarrassed.

He or she: 'It was no joke, I suppose . . . but it's over now, and you got through it in the end, and that's the main thing. Don't you agree, Sarah?'*

I'm trying to transcribe this story in the right order as far as possible, and I think it was at this point that Klara said:

'I didn't say any more. I looked at them intently. I don't know if it was hatred I felt, but as they were talking to me, both gabbling away as fast as they could, in those last minutes I made my decision. Without taking my eyes off them, I put my little case on the table and opened it so that the lid covered my hands and I could release the safety catch inside without being seen. They watched me without understanding what was going on, and I got the revolver out as fast as I could and killed them both, first him then her, all very very fast. He fell on the floor, and I gave him another bullet in the head; she collapsed on to the table, and she too got a bullet point-blank in the temple. Impossible that they should survive.

'Afterwards, I took the front door key from the shelf, it was my mother's, the key with the shiny little ring; the other one was in the lock. I locked the door from the inside, and took that key too. Then I went into the pantry, left one of the keys in plain view on the sideboard—it too was my mother's, with a shiny ring. That was all I took from the apartment—my mother's two keys. That's what

*Author's note: Under the Nazis, Jewis women had to register their first given name as 'Sarah'; for Jewish men, the first name had to be 'Israel'.

I had in my case, together with the revolver empty of bullets. I did have a fifth one left; I used it to kill a rat in a cellar where I slept.'

I only asked:

'Have you regretted it since?'

'No. Those people had plenty of good luck all through everything. I'm just their bad luck, the bomber, the falling flower-pot, the stray bullet, the interrupted burglar, just bad luck, that's all.'

She thought for a while.

'But I'm not bad luck just on my own. The bad luck was the meeting between their stupidity, egoism and hypocrisy, and me and my revolver. I hadn't come to kill them, I didn't know they were there, didn't know anything about what had happened. I just wanted to see the house again, it was a miracle that it was still standing. And to find your way anywhere in Berlin . . . it took me a week. I couldn't recognise anything, you had to be on your guard all the time, go through the ruins from one zone to another, the rubble, and rats everywhere, and ghosts—crazy, wild-looking folk who couldn't understand if you asked them a question . . . then to see this self-satisfied pair, shameless, almost resentful, above all shameless, inaccessible to the least shame or doubt—I'd have sensed the slightest flicker of uncertainty, the smallest chink in their armour . . . I wasn't asking much . . . so that was the bad luck—what they stood for and what I was at that particular moment.'

There was a short silence.

'They died sitting in their chairs.' (She corrected herself.) 'They died sitting in my German grandparents' Biedermeier chairs, digesting their dinner. What luxury! Very different from death on block 25. Very different from being gassed and incinerated.

'I gave them an easy death, the kind refused all those who were hanged, gassed or enslaved, who died in the most complete abjection, humiliation, and sordid fear. *Their* death wasn't disgusting. It was quick, with no apprehension, illness or suffering beforehand. To these despicable people, I gave what everyone hopes for. It's not fair, really.

'And,' she added, 'I even saved them from being put on trial, and from old age, illness and remorse. I delivered them from at least three of those calamities! If I have a regret, it's that I didn't act out of premeditation. It was an accident rather than a worthy deed.'

During the evening of that Saturday, while talking of this and that, she from time to time added a detail. For example, as well as the two keys, she took the contract of sale, which she later conscientiously burned. She also found her climbing boots in the lumber-room off the kitchen. I remember that lumber-room; we sometimes hid in there to play. There were two enormous cupboards and a hanging wardrobe, with skis, racquets, cricket gear, skittles, and all kinds of walking and sports shoes.

Klara confirmed that they hadn't changed anything,

except . . . except what they called the modern drawing-room . . . the small one . . . not a single item of its furniture or its other contents was left.

Margarethe had done over the room entirely with creations by her Bauhaus friends—furniture, carpets, lamps, hangings, two Klees, I think—in short, everything that Ullrich Adler hated.

She also told me that before she shut the front door, she examined the frame on both sides, and the lock. No sign of a break-in or repairs.

At first I couldn't see the significance of these details about the small drawing-room and the door. Later, I gradually guessed.

'Mother had a horror of weapons, she never knew nor wanted to know how to use them, she didn't like me going to the firing range with my father . . . She would have used poison . . . if, as you said, your mother got some for her . . . But with their sons and son-in-law in the Wehrmacht, *they* had guns . . . And then,' she concluded bitterly, 'such a big apartment for just one person, and in her situation, people thought that was funny . . .'

Then I understood.

She told me one of her plans had been to set fire to the building, and she went so far as to find a jerrican of petrol, but she remembered Fräulein Kuntz in time.

'So you see!' she commented.

I mentally finished the sentence with 'I'm not a monster.'
But she didn't say it.

And then, that last evening, before she went to bed, this:
'They called me Sarah—can you believe it?'

I didn't react.

Then she said something strange.

'It was they who released the safety catch of my revolver; Sarah was the trigger.'

'Are you telling me, Klara, it was all because of that name?'

'Yes, probably . . . the word "Jew" has done for plenty of others!'

How can one believe it . . . ought one to believe it? One must allow for Klara's delirious invention, her imagination, the possible transposition of her desires.

One ends up believing it.

Shutting the words up in a cupboard and throwing away the key, forgetting that either the key or the cupboard ever existed.

I see Klara as a building site, on which who can say what may be constructed?

www.vintage-books.co.uk